THE CLOCKWORK CITY

A STEAMPUNK ADVENTURE MYSTERY

LADY GEORGIA BRUNEL MYSTERIES
BOOK ONE

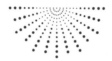

SHELLEY ADINA

Cover art by Jenny Zemanek. Images not from the author's collection used under license.

The Clockwork City / Shelley Adina—1st ed.

ISBN 978-1-950854-67-7 R032523

❀ Created with Vellum

PRAISE FOR SHELLEY ADINA

"Shelley Adina adds murder to her steampunk world for a mysteriously delicious brew! You'll love watching her intrepid heroine (and unexpected friends) bring justice to the Wild West while pursuing a quest of her own."

— VICTORIA THOMPSON, BESTSELLING
AUTHOR OF *MURDER IN THE BOWERY*

"Shelley Adina has brilliantly combined steampunk with the 'clockwork cozy' in this series in which a young painter solves mysteries. Best of all, the novels feature familiar characters I love from her bestselling Magnificent Devices series. I can't wait for the next book!"

— NANCY WARREN, USA TODAY BESTSELLING
AUTHOR

"I finished reading the last page and found myself already craving the next mystery in this addictive series."

— LORI ALDEN HOLUTA, AUTHOR OF THE
BRASSBRIGHT CHRONICLES

For Skully and Nancy,
who love Georgia as much as I do

THE CLOCKWORK CITY

CHAPTER ONE

TUESDAY, APRIL 30, 1895

The Duchy of Venice

*I*t's not too showy?"

In the vast bedroom of their villa, Georgia Brunel's aunt Millicent turned this way and that in the light pouring in through the three arched windows. Ah, the light of Venice. It picked out the quality of the lace trim on Millie's embroidered white blouse, the lines of the sweeping grey skirts and matching jacket with green soutache trim that concealed her too-thin figure, and the poufs of her faded blond hair, done up in the new high style upon which her feathered and beribboned hat would rest.

It also glinted on the anxiety in her eyes.

"Darling Millie," Georgia said with affection, "have you ever been accused of being showy in all your fifty-eight summers?"

"Please do not cast my age up to me. My point is, it doesn't do to draw attention, yet I've never owned clothes quite so fine as these. Thanks to you."

Georgia slipped an arm around the shoulders of her late husband's aunt, now her companion and closest friend, and squeezed. "It is unlikely anyone will notice us when His Majesty Umberto I and Queen Margherita di Savoia open the art exhibition. Particularly if she wears her diamonds."

Millie sniffed. "One should never wear diamonds before dinner." She looked Georgia up and down. "You look lovely, dear. The curls and crown of braids suit you very well, and this blue silk shantung brings out the depth of color in your eyes."

Georgia had rather thought so herself, but it did not do to say it aloud. "I know I am supposed to be wearing purple after a year in black, but I long for colors. And royal blue, you know, is not so far from purple as to be in poor taste."

"Purple makes both of us look sickly," Aunt Millie said with rather more honesty than tact. "This is perfect, and the cut of the walking costume sets off your figure admirably."

Georgia might be thirty-eight, and the mother of a newly minted Oxford scholar, but she had kept her figure through regular riding and exercise and a practical diet. Not for her the twelve courses and endless desserts so favored by the Prince of Wales's set. Those indulgences, and others, had hastened her husband's demise. Georgia took her example from the Queen and Prince Consort, who could dance most people under the table even at their ages.

Oh, to dance again!

They had come to enjoy the Esposizione Internazionale d'Arte del Città di Venezia at the insistence of darling Teddy. At nineteen, he might now be the fifth Baron Langford, but he was also a loving son who had no illusions about his father's character or the quality of her life at the latter's hands. Now that her year of mourning was over, he had practically pushed them out the door of their town house in Belgravia, handed her a letter from his banker that would finance years of peregrinations, and commanded her to enjoy herself.

And, thorough child that he was, a second letter had been delivered at the airfield at Hampstead Heath, should she not have thought he was serious.

Dearest Mama,

I hope this note finds you in time at the Hampstead Heath airfield, no doubt looking forward to boarding HMAS Juno in Paris and enjoying the flight to Venice. What a pity it lasts only a day ... I hear Juno is the last word in long-distance airship travel. I hope you talk the captain into allowing you to pilot it, even if only for a few minutes. Not many fellows could say that their mother had flown the mightiest vessel in the skies! Not many fellows can say their mother can fly anything at all, come right down to it. I am glad that mine can, as easily as she pilots a steam landau.

You deserve this voyage, Mama. While my feelings for my late father are a disorganized mess, chief among them is happiness that you can now spend his money in whatever manner you please. There is plenty to go round—enough to fund an excursion to the Antipodes, if that is your desire! Perhaps you ought to buy your own ship, now that I have mine. I know I must register her without delay, but I am still dithering over her name. I am counting on making friends who will help with this most pressing problem.

I hope you will enjoy your painting lessons in your Venetian villa, and that you manage to have an adventure or two along the way. I want at least two letters a week, and I will hold you to it! Tell Great-Aunt Millie that one of her pullets has laid a topping brown egg and I made my breakfast of it. I go back up to Oxford on

Wednesday, and wish I could conceal her among my luggage (the hen, not my aunt).

Hodges is here for our final ride about the estate, so I must close.
Your loving son
Theodore

Teddy would be happy to learn they had indeed had an adventure—within a day of his letter, to boot. After a rather difficult flight in which Millie might have lost her life had it not been for Georgia, they had landed at the airfield on the Lido last week. They had taken up a month's residence in one of the villas just off the Grand Canal that had belonged to the Falier family in the seventeenth century. The reason Georgia had taken it was delightfully obvious as she and Millie descended the grand staircase—from floor to ceiling the walls of the Villa dei Pappagalli had been painted with murals of its namesake parrots. Any house that could greet its guests with such joy and beauty was a house in which she was delighted to stay. The fact that it came with a staff and a cook only added to its many superiorities.

The staff included a young gondolier named Lorenzo, grandson of Signore and Signora Airone, the majordomo and cook. The young man bowed as they made their way down the water stairs punctually at eleven thirty. He handed them into their seats, and then pushed off, the gondola swimming like a graceful black fish into the stream of vessels on the Grand Canal. Most of Venice, it seemed, was on its way to see the opening of the exhibition.

The grand event was to be held in the gardens of what had once been a convent, Lorenzo told them. "Everything in Venice was once something else," he said rather sadly. He was learning English at school and was happy to practice. "But we respect our past and do our best in the present. Will this suit your ladyship? Er, this er—"

"We call it a jetty. *Grazie,* Lorenzo." Georgia might be fluent in French and German, but her studies had not extended to Italian. Oh, she could say *please* and *thank you* and *what is the time*, but anything beyond that she must leave to Millie, who, besides Italian, also spoke fluent Spanish. Between them, they would be able to communicate with anyone from queen to cook on this trip, if called upon.

And who knew? They might wash up on the shores of South America yet. Or anywhere else that fancy took them.

Lorenzo promised to return for them when the bells rang four o'clock, and they made their way through the gates. "Isn't it lovely?" Millie breathed. "Look, trees! The first I've seen in Venice." Under the precious trees, white pavilions had been pitched to house the paintings, the former now standing on the ends of their ropes like butterflies waiting to lift. Flowers made bright ribbons along the paths, which were of white gravel. In the distance, an orchestra played, the sun sparkling off flutes and trumpets.

They were playing the national anthem.

"Goodness. We must hurry," Georgia said. "I don't expect to shake Their Majesties' hands, but we ought to arrive on time, at least."

"You did send a card to the palace," Millie reminded her. "The queen is acquainted with Countess Dunsmuir, and you are related to the Dunsmuirs through your mother. Such connections are not to be discounted. They may indeed wish you to be known to them."

"I shall take your optimism as a compliment and no more.

5

I am quite looking forward to the ball, however. Come, over by that little hornbeam. We shall have both shade and a splendid view."

Their Majesties were pleased to declare the exhibition open and to welcome all their visitors to Venice. Of particular notice was a group of schoolchildren, holding hands in a chain and escorted by nuns. Millie smiled as she translated. "The queen has just opened a library for the blind, and these children are among the first to enjoy it. She is known, I am told, for her activity and charity."

"Then I salute her," Georgia said as the royal lady bent to shake hands with the children. She was slightly more stout than Princess Alexandra, and had clearly been brought up with the same standards as Millie. There was not a diamond in sight except for the one on her left hand.

"Lady Langford?" said a voice behind them. "Can it be you?"

Georgia turned in surprise to see a man of about her own age, holding the hand of a girl who looked to be about ten. "Why ... it is Sir Francis Thorne, is it not? And this must be your daughter—Cora, was it?"

"What a good memory you have," he said with a smile and a courtly bow. "We have not seen one another since the house party at Blenheim, just before—" He stopped, no doubt thinking it indelicate to refer to Hart's death.

Cora bobbed a shy curtsey, and Georgia shook off the appalling memory of that unfortunate house party to introduce them both to Millie.

"I am here in my professional capacity as a diplomat," Sir Francis went on, straightening with pride. "You may have heard that I specialize in bringing countries together in the development of technologies that improve the lives of us all."

She had not. "My goodness, what a responsibility. And Lady Thorne?" Georgia inquired politely. "Is she enjoying the exhibition?"

A shadow flitted through Sir Francis's smiling eyes. "My wife did not join us on this trip. She remains at home in Munich."

Cora tilted her chin. "Mama could not be spared by Empress Christina," she said proudly. "She is working on an automaton specifically commissioned, to say nothing of the breakwaters that will be used in—"

"Cora, my darling, I am quite certain that Lady Langford and Miss Brunel are not interested in the contents of your mother's laboratory," Sir Francis said with a chuckle. "To say nothing of the fact that her tinkers and toys are not to be discussed in public."

Cora blushed scarlet and when she ducked her head, tears glimmered on her lashes at the rebuke. "I beg your pardon, your ladyship," she whispered.

"On the contrary," Georgia said gently to the top of the daisy-crowned straw hat. "I am the mother of a tinkerer myself, and am quite familiar with the contents of benches and laboratories. The only difference is that Lord Langford is not quite so likely to have state secrets cluttering up the corners of his. Not yet, at any rate. I have heard, you see, of the high regard in which Lady Thorne is held in such circles."

"I read that she is to join Lady Claire and Sir Andrew Malvern themselves at a symposium in London in the late summer," Millie put in. "It is a most exclusive company, the papers say."

Cora's spirits had bloomed once more. "Indeed it is," she said eagerly. "I only hope that I may go along. It is lucky they scheduled the event before school begins, isn't it? Otherwise I should never hope to—"

"Cora," her father said, glancing apologetically at his companions. "Have you been putting chatter powder in your *cioccolata calda* again?"

The poor child wilted. "No, Papa."

Had he no regard for the feelings and thoughts of his daughter, to squash her in public this way? Georgia had half a mind to invite her to come along for a cone of gelato—ladies only—to hear more about her mother's work.

But Sir Francis forestalled her. "Are you attending the ball this evening, Lady Langford?"

"We have been invited," Millie said.

But he did not seem to hear. Instead, he gazed into Georgia's eyes. "I will be quite unhappy if you do not come," he said. "May I be so bold as to secure the first waltz?"

Georgia smothered her surprise and resisted the urge to step back. "If we arrive in time," she said airily. "I expect that, with Their Majesties in attendance, it will be an impossible crush."

"I am a determined man, Lady Langford," he said. "I shall find you though thousands bar the way."

Dear me. Had he been this flirtatious at Blenheim? She couldn't remember.

"What a pity your wife was not able to accompany you," Millie said coolly, bringing herself more firmly to the man's attention. "Then you might have enjoyed the first waltz with her."

When he only smiled weakly, accepting the rebuke,

Georgia turned once more to Cora. "I hope you will enjoy the exhibition," she said. "Miss Brunel and I are supposed to be embarking upon a painting holiday. My son felt that it ought to commence with inspiration of the sort to be found here. I am an appalling painter, but I must do his optimism justice."

"That cannot be so, ma'am," she said softly, her eyes flicking to her father as though to confirm she still had permission to speak. "Every lady is educated in dancing, music, and painting, is she not?"

"She is if her talents lie in that direction," Georgia said. "Mine seem to go galumphing off after mathematics, logic, and geometry. And horses. Terribly unladylike, unless one rides to hounds. Which I do, though my sympathies lie entirely with the fox. Such a trial I was to my mother, rest her soul."

The smile had returned to Cora's face, and a dimple had appeared just at the corner of her mouth. Georgia felt a pang deep in her chest, as though her heart had squeezed. Helena would have been just Cora's age if she had not—if she—

No, she must not think of it. Not here, in the sunshine of Italy, in full view of half of Europe.

Millie must have sensed something of her distress, for she took Georgia's arm. "Lovely to meet you, Miss Thorne. Sir Francis, we shall look forward to seeing you this evening. Enjoy the exhibition, both of you. Good afternoon."

Georgia went willingly. Or perhaps willy-nilly might be more accurate, for she came to herself under a fluttering set of canvas triangles that formed the roof of a small pavilion, gazing blindly at an oil painting of Saluté silhouetted by a sunset whose colors were surely not found in nature.

"Are you quite all right, dear?" Millie murmured.

9

"Yes. Thank you. It is only that—" She could not finish.

"I know." Millie had been there that night, eleven years ago. Had sponged away Georgia's tears. And the blood. And, finally, had wrapped in a soft blanket the little being who would never draw breath because of her father's violence, and taken her away.

Georgia squared her shoulders. "I must have a palate cleanser after this sunset. May we visit the watercolors?"

The beauty that others had created refreshed her spirits, as did a cone of pistachio gelato and a glass of lemonade. They did not see Sir Francis or Cora again, but they did see any number of her acquaintances from England and the Continent.

They spent a restorative half hour with the Comtesse de Valmy—née Anne MacLeod from Edinburgh, an old schoolmate—who vacillated between a watercolor of the Grand Canal and another of some ancient, mossy sequoias painted *en plein air* in the Columbia Territory. The visit ended with the sequoias and an invitation to tea at *le comte*'s villa on the Grand Canal, to say nothing of a promise to visit the château sooner rather than later.

And then there was Ernst von Zeppelin, a cousin of the Count of airship fame. A friend of Hart's. But she could not hold that against him. He was a lovely man, his wife charming, and their six children … well, she didn't actually meet them. They had, he and his wife confessed with a laughing look of alarm, lost them at the gates. But he was quite confident they would turn up before dark.

By four o'clock she was pathetically happy to see Lorenzo and the gondola, and made no objection when Millie insisted on naps for them both before dinner and the ball.

Not even Millie knew of the tears that wet her pillow.

GEORGIA MONTGOMERY HAD BEEN an eighteen-year-old heiress when she'd first laid eyes on Hartford Brunel at a country house party. It had been one of the first events of her come-out year, and she had not been experienced enough to understand what she'd once heard her Aunt Maud say: "He was one of those dashing, wicked young men who soon leave off being young and dashing, and keep on being wicked." She, dazzled by the Brunel family fame and enchanted by his choosing her above all others, had fallen fathoms deep in love.

Hartford had not objected to marrying her, and her dowry had sealed the deal. Decades ago, in 1819 her grandfather had saved the Tinkering Prince's life during the Congress of Vienna, and in gratitude His Royal Highness had given him lands in the north of England. Their sheep had turned out to be grazing placidly above several rich veins of coal, which made the family fortune.

She and Hart had gone to Bavaria for a month's honeymoon, and she had come back disillusioned and pregnant. She had learned to hide the bruises, especially when Teddy grew old enough to ask about them. She had left off wearing short sleeves, then sharing her husband's bedroom, and finally, being alone with him at all.

After Helena's premature birth, Georgia had passed through the valley of death, but had managed to climb out the other side through grim determination that Teddy should not be left alone with his father. Millie had been staying at Langford Park, and between the two of them, they had contrived it so that for years, the baron's aunt was always on the point of going, but never quite achieving it. For in Millicent Brunel, Georgia had found not only a friend and companion, but a second mother, too.

Millie had no illusions about her nephew. She had no illusions about life in general, being the maiden aunt passed from member to member of a family too proud to admit that any of them could be homeless.

Then, last year, on his way home to Langford Park from an evening at a neighboring estate, Hartford had drunkenly miscalculated a jump, setting his horse at a fallen log across the path without realizing half the tree and its thick branches still remained above. He had been knocked unconscious from the saddle, and then the panicked horse had bolted. With Hart's foot twisted in one stirrup, he had been dragged some two miles through woods and fields. Their steward had found the horse grazing on the lawn the next morning, his late master still suspended from one side.

Georgia had spent that day shivering on the sofa in her room, Millie plying her with tea and shortbread, unable to believe that she was free. Every hymn at the funeral had been a song of praise and tears under her voluminous black veil. Every day that she put on her widow's weeds prompted a prayer of thanks. And when her year of mourning was ended, she gently laid her black garments away in tissue paper, and ordered new clothes.

Every ball gown had short sleeves. Two of them had only delicious flutters of lace that could hardly be counted as sleeves at all.

Theodore Isambard Montgomery Brunel, fifth Baron Langford, inherited a fortune. For as much as she hated Hartford, Georgia was forced to admit that he was no wastrel. He had a flair for money, did not gamble, and believed in progress. Teddy had inherited these traits, as well as her love of horses and her logical mind. He was taking a degree in engineering, and once it was in hand, planned further study in civil engineering at the University of Edinburgh. He dreamed of emulating his famous relative and building a tunnel, not under the Thames, but under the English Channel, from Dover to Calais.

Her darling boy. The apple of her eye. She had no doubt he would accomplish it.

On this happy thought, she must have dozed, for the next thing she knew, Millie was touching her shoulder.

"Time to wake up, dearest, or we shall be late for the ball."

CHAPTER TWO

8:30 P.M.

The palace of the Doge, the elected duke who ruled Venice, had been given over to Their Majesties to entertain as they pleased. Tonight it pleased them to preside over the ball marking the opening of the exhibition.

"Goodness me," Millie remarked as they moved through the receiving line, "there are so many diamonds on display it is a wonder we do not throw the great gearworks beneath the city off balance and tip ourselves into the lagoon."

"I am disappointed the neighborhoods have not moved since we have been here," Georgia murmured. "We shall simply have to stay until they do."

Four hundred years before, the Doge then in power had been in such fear for his life from his many enemies that he had commissioned the inventor Leonardo da Vinci to solve the problem. The great mathematician and engineer had installed a massive clockwork beneath the city, with platforms bearing up the many neighborhoods on their islands. The church bells would ring, the bridges would go up, and the neighborhoods would slowly revolve into new positions, thus confounding anyone in search of the Doge.

He must not have lived in this palace, Georgia thought, for its domes and towers were visible from nearly every vantage point in the city.

They reached Their Majesties and sank into curtsies as they were announced.

"Welcome, welcome," the king said, clearly already exhausted and confining his remarks to the bare necessities.

"What a lovely gown, Lady Langford," the queen said, sharp eyes taking in every detail of the cream chiffon and lace of Georgia's neckline that softened the severity of the silk. "The latest from London? What do you call such a color?"

"Midnight blue, Your Majesty."

"A perfect match for the sapphires."

"Thank you, Your Majesty." Georgia dipped into another curtsey and they were free to escape into the ballroom. "I don't think she liked my dress," she said to Millie.

"There is rather a lot of decolleté, dear."

"The necklace covers most of it. And people in glass houses showing just as much decolleté ought not to throw stones."

"I think she believed you to be still in mourning."

Oh. "Well, it is not likely we shall see each other again. But you do look splendid, Millie, dear. Have you put on a pound? It was that delicious pasta with the squid ink Cook prepared for supper, wasn't it?"

"We will not discuss my weight in the ballroom, if you please. Besides, here is Sir Francis, as promised."

Georgia sighed and offered her hand. He bowed over it, as

happy to see her as if she had been a present on Christmas morning. Georgia made a persistent point of bringing up Lady Thorne throughout the whole of their waltz. And through the polka, though in shorter sentences. She declined the schottische altogether as being far too likely to enable conversation, and whirled away instead in the arms of the Conte di Narboni, whose family owned the largest palazzo on the Grand Canal.

Outside of Sir Francis, Georgia was enjoying herself. There was no shortage of partners, and no one seemed to think anything of married men dancing with widows or ingenues or their wives, so long as the marble floor was full. To her delight, she found herself waltzing with Sir Frederic Leighton, one of whose paintings hung in the morning room at Langford Park.

"There are several of us daubers here," he told her, his cheeks flushed with pleasure at her compliments. "We have been imported by the Doge to attract people to the exhibition —myself, Millais, Burne-Jones and one or two Impressionists. I would object to being advertising if I were not so inspired by *La Serenissima* herself. I say, Lady Langford, have you ever considered modeling?"

She laughed and gave his impeccable evening jacket a playful tap as they went into another turn. "Certainly not, sir. And you must not say such things. People will think me fast."

"Then I must carry your face in my memory. You have more than mere beauty, my dear. You are *interesting*."

Such a delightful man.

Her next partner was a friend of his, introduced as Mr Dustin Seacombe. He was not quite so delightful, but she did not discover that until halfway through the first measure, when he trod on her foot.

"I apologize, my lady," he said in a voice like rocks grinding together deep in a cave. His appearance was extraordinary to begin with—a handlebar moustache, a waistcoat made of what looked to be canvas, and his coat—

Georgia looked away. When he'd removed it to dance, she'd seen that not only was it made of tanned leather and fell below his knees, but it was slit up the back as though meant for riding. Three capes fell over the shoulders to keep out the weather. Did he expect a hurricane at Their Majesties' ball?

"Think nothing of it," she said politely. "I have another foot."

His gaze settled on her face as though humor were cause for suspicion. "You must excuse my manners. In the Texican Territory, we don't see a lot of shindigs like this."

Shindigs, evidently, meant balls. Or barn dances. Or both.

"You are rather far from home."

"I am," he agreed, but did not elaborate. "And you?"

"Only England. We sailed on *Juno* last week. Only a day to cross Europe. It seems amazing to me, but then, I have not traveled much."

"It's three days on *Persephone* to New York. A lot of water in that pond. Couple more days from there to Santa Fe."

She would have replied if he had not caught her skirt under his boot heel.

Boots! In a ballroom!

He steadied her before resuming the lead. "I beg your pardon, my lady."

"My fault entirely. My train is not long, but clearly this wrist loop is inadequate to its task."

"Maybe I ought to quit while I'm ahead."

"You may not have a choice, Mr Seacombe. It appears Sir Francis Thorne wishes to cut in. Again."

He must have heard the sigh in her tone. "Want me to tell him to skedaddle?"

It took a moment to translate this in her head. "While I am in favor of that in principle, in reality it will not do to cause a scene."

"You've already danced with him twice. None of my business, but if you were my sister, I wouldn't advise encouraging him. He's one to take risks. Word is he's up to his eyes in debt to one of the cabinet ministers."

Stricken silent with surprise, she lost her opportunity to escape.

"May I cut in?" Sir Francis smiled at her as though her acceptance were a foregone conclusion.

"This dance ain't over." Mr Seacombe's growl raised the hairs on the back of Georgia's neck.

"Sir, being from the Fifteen Colonies, you might not be aware that it is customary at occasions such as this—"

But Mr Seacombe had already whirled her away in a pair of masterful turns that miraculously left her hems and the toes of her slippers intact.

"I do not know whether to thank you or cut you dead," she said breathlessly.

"Where I come from, that last means something quite different from what it does here."

"Yes, well, the end result is often the same."

"The Fifteen Colonies," he said with a snort at Sir Francis. "Can't the man tell a Texican on sight?"

"Evidently not." Georgia would not have been able to, either, but she was not likely to forget her first lesson. "Mr

Seacombe, here comes the Conte di Narboni. I beg you to allow him to cut in. We are acquainted and he is second cousin to Her Majesty. You must not insult him."

"As you like, my lady."

She breathed a sigh of relief as the count claimed her without difficulty. The clock struck midnight, at which point she realized that Sir Francis was bent on causing a scene no matter how well-behaved she or her partners were. He cut in *again*, which made the dear count swell up like a plum and lose his temper. Had this been England, there might have been a freezing silence and remarks at gentlemen's clubs. Its being Italy, there was a lot of shouting and some airborne glassware.

However, she didn't actually see it, only heard it. For by that time, Millie had abandoned the aide-de-camp with whom she was dancing and had hustled Georgia out of the ballroom.

"Italy!" Shaking her head, Millie fastened her opera cloak and tugged her gloves higher on her arms as they descended the palace steps.

"Italy," Georgia said on a dreamy sigh, unable to decide whether the evening had been a delight or a disaster.

She had expected they would have to walk back to their villa, but the resourceful Lorenzo swanned up in the gondola, waving to get their attention. Georgia settled back against the cushions and let the sounds of the ball fade into the distance.

She had never been the cause of flung glassware before. Only the target.

All in all, she concluded, the ball had been rather a delight.

Wednesday, May 1, 1895

GEORGIA ROSE at eight the next morning determined to make Teddy proud, and attempt a watercolor painting. Since they had left the ball relatively early, she had slept well and deeply. She must not get into the habit of keeping country hours, however. She set up her little travel easel on the balcony, a cup of something frothy called a *cappuccino* at her elbow, and realized that the morning light was its own reward.

She could see why dear Sir Frederic loved to paint here.

Swiftly, she sketched the arch of the bridge to her right, and the shapes of one or two gondolas tied to blue-and-white striped poles. These lay in front of narrow villas whose lacy stone balconies would, she could see already, provide a challenge.

The next hour was spent in a happy attempt to replicate the way the shadows fell under the bridge, and the ripples of color the painted villas made in the water. She resisted the urge to overpaint, especially since the toothy paper did not seem inclined to dry as quickly as she had anticipated. The air, despite its warmth, was as full of moisture as any fen in Norfolk.

She left the little painted sketch to dry on a table in the sunny sitting room, and took her equipment downstairs. There was an enchanting door on the opposite side of the canal with hanging baskets of flowers on either side that she must capture from water level. No reflections there, just simple shapes and shadows and a chance to paint the raucous reds of geraniums and impatiens against the yellow stucco.

Last night, when Lorenzo had poled them in, the water stairs had been nearly engulfed by the tide; this morning, as she went out through the French doors, they were half exposed on the ebb. And—goodness—what on earth?

Georgia's mind took a moment to parse what it was seeing. Then she dropped her easel and paintbox on the *fondamente*, hauled up her skirts, and descended four steps green and glistening with slippery weed.

The body of a man floated over the bottom-most steps, which were still submerged yet clear in the undulating light. Close by, where a short stone jetty waited to receive supplies for the household, an abandoned gondola bumped the stone with a forlorn, hollow sound.

The man lay face down, his arms floating out to both sides. He wore evening dress—black coat, a glimpse of the back of a white collar, black trousers. No shoes. Dark hair.

Spots floated in front of her eyes, and not from the sparkling sunlight on the water, either. She dragged in several deep breaths until her vision cleared.

Turn him over to see who he is.

No, she could not bear it.

But he is floating on my water stairs. Did he come to see us and meet with an accident?

He could have got the wrong address.

But the houses in Venice had no addresses. There was no point, since the neighborhoods changed location. And there were hardly any streets, only canals and flagstone lanes. People went to the post office for their post. It was not delivered via pneumatic tube, as it was in London.

Oh, how she wished she were in London right now, and not standing over the dead body of an unfortunate man!

Get hold of yourself, Georgia.

Another breath calmed the incipient panic. She apologized

to the unknown man for deserting him at such a time, and hurried inside, calling for help.

The housemaid appeared instantly, took one look out of the French doors, and screamed.

Georgia grabbed her by the shoulders, which made the girl gasp into silence. "We must call the police. Do you understand? The police!"

"P-p-polizia?"

"Si, the polizia. At once! Pronto!"

The housemaid scurried away, wailing.

The minutes ticked by with excruciating slowness on the small chronometer pinned to the lapel of her linen waistcoat. Georgia had time to drag Millie downstairs to witness the scene, and it was she who helped Georgia pick up her scattered painting equipment. Georgia's hands shook so badly that she dropped the pot of Alizarin Crimson altogether and wept as she tried to scrape the precious pigment back into the pot. She would never paint the geraniums opposite now.

In fact, she thought grimly as she scrubbed the paint off her hands in her water closet, for tuppence she would tell Millie to pack and they would board an airship to Switzerland. The south of France. Anywhere but here.

A commotion in the hall brought the two of them down from the first-floor sitting room, to find their majordomo showing the police through to the water stairs. Signore Airone was a man of dignity and duty, and it was clear that a dead body on his premises was more than he could bear. His English was adequate for the requirements of the household, but when asked, he was simply not up to translating questions from the police in his state of mind.

Millie did so in Italian, rapidly and with colloquial accuracy, though Georgia was aware that the Venetian dialect was beyond her.

"Who discovered the body?" the taller, thinner man in the black coat and trousers asked.

"I did," Georgia said. "I came downstairs to paint, and found him floating there, as you see him."

"At what time?"

"About half past nine, I believe. The tide had uncovered four of the steps, if that is helpful."

All of them crowded outside on the stone *fondamente* as though the position of the tide upon the steps were a vital piece of evidence. For all she knew, it was.

"Seven are uncovered," the shorter one said. It sounded like an accusation. As though she had lied about there being four.

"You did take your time arriving," Georgia pointed out.

Whether Millie couched this observation in politer terms or not, it was clear the policeman didn't appreciate the remark.

"And what is this?" He pointed at the crimson stain upon the *fondamente*. "Is it blood? The victim's blood?"

"Certainly not," Millie said indignantly. "Her ladyship spilled some of her paint in the shock of finding that gentleman."

"So you say," he said, bending to examine the stain, which bore the evidence of Georgia's attempts first to scrape up the pigment, and then to wash the remainder from the stone with canal water.

Both attempts had been clumsy and unsuccessful and now, she realized, could be construed as the acts of a guilty person.

Which was ridiculous.

"Oh, please," she begged, "won't you take him out of the water? He must have family or friends who will be worried that he has not come home."

"It is better that we wait for the monks," the tall one said.

"The who?" Millie blurted. "Whatever for?"

Signore Airone pulled himself together enough to recall his duty. "The monasteries house our hospitals, Signorina. When there is a death, they come and bear the body away to be washed and tended before the funeral."

"Oh, but you mustn't do that," Georgia said, looking from one man to another. "Not until we know how he died." All three male faces took on expressions of disgust. She realized a moment too late that she had sounded not only unladylike, but ghoulish, too. "He may have met with an accident," she amended lamely. "His family will wish to know."

"Or he may have met with murder," the tall policeman said, his hooded eyes intent upon her. "We will make it our business to find out."

She and Millie were both rendered speechless by the implication.

"But in the meanwhile, perhaps we may indeed pull him out and lay him upon the *fondamente* as a courtesy to *i monaci*," the short one said. He seemed to be in charge. "Signore, that oar, if you please."

An oar floated beside the little jetty—the long black sort used by the gondoliers.

"Surely a man in evening dress did not steer the gondola himself," Millie said in English.

"Perhaps he was a Venetian," Georgia said. "Could he have lost it when he fell out of the gondola?"

Signore Airone glanced at her while the policemen used

24

the oar to bring the man closer to the steps. "Many men have the skill of gondoliers, Signorina. It is expected, in a city with streets of water. Our boys learn early how to steer and pole around their neighborhoods."

But was he a resident of Venice? Somehow Georgia did not think so. It could not be the cut of his coat that gave her this impression, for it was mostly submerged.

How strange.

Millie did not translate the remarks of the policemen as they hauled the body from the water and staggered with it up the wet steps. It was only when they laid it face up upon the stone, rivulets of water running from it and their own trouser legs, that Georgia gasped in horror.

She had assumed the victim was not Venetian because some part of her mind had recognized him.

"Signora?" the policeman said sharply. "Do you know this man?"

Words would not come, so she merely nodded. Her chest seemed to have been pulled in like a drawstring, squeezing her lungs so that she could not breathe.

Millie croaked, "We do know him. He attended Their Majesties' ball last night, as did we. It is Sir Francis Thorne."

CHAPTER THREE

*O*ver the last six years, Millicent Brunel had come to
believe that Georgia might be a force to be reckoned
with if only she could be brought to believe in her own worth
and talents. Lady Langford amused herself by behaving like
other women of her class—painting holidays being a case in
point—and by adhering to the rules of society as though by
doing so, she would be rewarded with a generous helping of
happiness.

It had not worked the first time, though Millie had to
admit that the subsequent arrival of Teddy Brunel in the
world had been worth the sacrifices. Even Georgia would not
hesitate to say so, despite the heavy price she had paid.

As a young woman, Millie had concluded that once one
recognized that the rules existed, one might see how they
could be thwarted. Bent. Paid homage to and then ignored, if
it came to that. She had no doubt that Georgia was fast
coming up on such a realization. The royal blue walking
costume and last night's decolletage were merely the first
indications of a change in the wind.

She might at this moment be looking at another.

"Wait." Georgia held up an imperious hand and Millie prepared herself to translate.

The two policeman looked up, one of them squeezing the water from his linen trouser legs and swearing under his breath.

"Aren't you going to examine Sir Francis for signs of injury?"

"That is for the monks to do, Signora," the shorter one said.

"If a man is going to die on my doorstep, then I insist upon knowing what happened," she said with admirable firmness. "Have neither of you read Sir Arthur Conan Doyle?"

The barely concealed distaste with which they had greeted her first suggestion of an examination congealed into loathing at the mention of the great man's name.

"We do not conduct our investigations like characters in penny novels," the short one snapped. "If you touch this man's body, I will have you charged with disturbing the dead."

"The penalty for most crimes in Venice, including that one, is a month under water," the tall one added with quite unnecessary venom.

Venom aside, Millie could not have heard correctly. *"Sott'acqua?"*

"Si, Signorina. In the Duchy, there is only one sentence for a person judged guilty of a crime. The severity is only a matter of length. They are assigned to the work crews under water, cleaning the great gearworks that have made our city famous."

Millie stared in horror at the water lapping at the last step. Her imagination failed her. "A month?" she repeated.

"Those who commit more serious crimes are sentenced to a year. Few survive that long." The tall policeman was enjoying this far too much. "If they do, they have learned their lesson and are released. *La Serenissima* is fortunate to have very few repeat offenders."

"Grazie, Signore," Millie managed. "I am grateful for your willingness to educate us, mere women and foreigners as we are."

This bit of flummery seemed to mollify them. Silence fell upon their vigil over poor Sir Francis. Though it must be said that while Georgia did not touch the gentleman, she examined every aspect of his form as best she could while she stood there, hands folded in front of her like a penitent in church.

Four monks arrived a quarter of an hour later, each holding the corner of a bier, and respectfully laid Sir Francis upon it. The policemen followed them out as Signore Airone made the sign of the cross over their threshold.

In the lane, the short one turned. "You spoke of the victim's family. Next of kin must be notified. Are they in the city?"

Georgia had not accompanied them, so Millie was forced to reply. "His wife is in Bavaria. In Munich. And there is a young daughter here. But I am afraid I do not know where either one lives."

"We will notify the embassy to send for the wife. Arrangements must be made."

Millie watched them long enough to be certain they would not return, before she went back out to the water stairs.

Georgia was up on the little stone jetty, the black oar in both hands, attempting to bring the abandoned gondola closer.

"My dear, what are you doing?" Millie didn't know whether to stop her or assist her. How many sets of eyes were already watching from behind lace curtains and carved stone balconies?

"I am gathering evidence in the best Doyle tradition."

With the oar wedged under the plank that served as a passenger seat—no cushions and gold leaf here—Georgia was able to float the gondola to the water stairs. This was no dory, light and mobile. It was far too heavy and large to drag up the stairs, even if they had wanted to. But they could tie it to the ring set in the *fondamente* and examine it at close range.

"What would Sir Arthur think of this?" Millie murmured. She had enormous admiration for the man and had even gone to several of his lectures. She and Georgia read each of his books aloud to each other, turn about, much to Teddy's amusement. But something about them satisfied both Georgia's orderly mind and Millie's need to know what prompted violence in the human heart.

Bending over the gondola next to Georgia and peering in, Millie quoted the great man's opening remarks at the latest lecture she had attended. "Every murder has a reason. Every murderer leaves something of himself behind."

"The former is likely true in this case," Georgia agreed. "But the latter? All I see is an empty boat."

That was all Millie saw, too. "Ours seems luxurious in comparison."

"I'll wager that any gondolier would be able to tell ours from any other on the canals, even if Lorenzo were not at the helm. But one that is completely plain? How many of those do you suppose ply the waters?"

"Dozens," Millie said. "Has it no identifying marks at all?" She could see none. Did scratches count?

"Even if it did, Sir Francis might have hailed it as easily as one hails a hansom cab in London, or boards a steambus."

"That prompts the question—if he did hail it, where is the gondolier? Did he kill Sir Francis and flee? If so, why?"

"There must have been a gondolier," Georgia said, straightening. "For I will bet the deed to Langford Park that Sir Francis Thorne has not been here in Venice taking lessons in how to propel a gondola."

"Lessons." Millie got to her feet. "Goodness me. I have just now recollected Cora Thorne."

Her own concern dawned in Georgia's face, too. "Oh, Millie. The police might tell her of her father's death, but is anyone in the household able to offer comfort?"

"Even if someone has, a child cannot stay alone in a strange city." Being alone was frightening enough at the age of twenty—or forty—never mind ten. "We do not even know if she has a governess or companion."

"Sir Francis never mentioned it. Such a dear child. We must go and ascertain her situation at once," Georgia said. "I have his card somewhere. My pocketbook, I think."

They left the gondola tied up and the oar drying on the *fondamente*, and fetched their hats. Telling Signore Airone that they would return in time for lunch, they had just sent for Lorenzo when every church bell in the neighborhood rang a peal.

Millie clapped her hands over her ears.

Every bell in the city was ringing. Insistent. Urgent.

"The bridges!" Georgia exclaimed. "The bells are the signal they're about to go up! We must watch, Millie."

She dashed across the hall and out to the water stairs, where they were just in time to see a pair of boys fling themselves off the little bridge across their canal and on to the *fondamente*. A scant second later, the bridge split in the middle, tilted toward the sky, and with a whirr of clockwork and the groaning of pulleys, the two halves seated themselves in some kind of submerged structure at the base.

And then—

"Ohhhh." The ground seemed to swing out from under Millie.

Georgia tottered sideways, grabbed her, and pulled her down to sit upon their own *fondamente*. The world seemed to lurch out—away—back again—the sky looped and spun—and then everything came to a grinding halt.

"The geraniums are gone," Georgia said inanely, staring across the canal at the unfamiliar view. "Bother. Is it over?"

"My goodness," Millie said, trying to catch her breath. "It is like the end of the world."

"Let us hope not." Georgia got up and offered her hand. "I suppose one learns to reach for the nearest post or door handle, and keep one's feet somehow. I take back what I said about wanting to see it. If that does not happen again before we leave, I shall be happy indeed."

What a good thing they had tied up the abandoned gondola. If they hadn't, it would have washed away in the churning movement. Everything architectural about their villa seemed to be still in its place. And here came Lorenzo, working the oar so that he nosed up to the jetty, since the water in front of the stairs was occupied by the plainer vessel.

"Beg pardon, ladies, but why is that old wreck in my way?"

"It is evidence in a police investigation," Millie told him.

31

"Her ladyship found a man's body on our stairs this morning—*i monaci* left with him just before the bridges went up."

Astonishment made his face go slack, and then it scrunched into disappointment. "I miss *every*thing."

"We must keep it here until the owner is located," Georgia said, climbing gingerly into his gondola.

"That won't be difficult—Paolo Barcaiolo will know. He owns the *fabbrica gondole* by the Accademia Bridge. All of Venice's *gondole* are made there."

It had not occurred to Millie that gondolas could be made in what amounted to a manufactory. But of course they must.

The young man steered them out into the canal.

Georgia said, "Lorenzo, could you take that gondola to him and have it identified for us? We must know who it belongs to. Then bring it back?"

"Certainly, Signora. But where are you going now?"

"To the house of Sir Francis Thorne." She handed up the card, and he looked at it for a moment before returning it.

"Castello, near the exhibition. He must be a rich man. We will have to ask from there, since the—"

"—bridges just went up," Millie finished with him simultaneously.

"At least you didn't fall in," Lorenzo said cheerfully. "We are always pulling tourists out of the canals. Don't they see the rings set into the walls? They're not for tying up horses, are they?"

The only horses Millie had seen here were of the bronze variety, commemorating generals and kings. Dead ones, of course.

The thought kept her silent all the way to the house of Sir

Francis. How, she wondered, would he be remembered by those who knew him?

~

LORENZO, among his many other talents, seemed to possess a gift for locating houses. Disembarking at its water stairs, Georgia knocked on the canal-side door of the villa rented by Sir Francis, and she and Millie were shown in. Like their own, the water-level floor had been used for commerce at one time, and was now a kind of receiving hall. They were asked to wait, and seated themselves in a pleasant grouping of chairs and sofas.

A cry issued from upstairs, and in a moment they heard a clatter of feet. Two people ran into the room—Cora Thorne, and pursuing her, a woman in a cap and apron who clearly functioned as a nanny.

"Do you have news of Papa?" the girl said, flinging herself on to the sofa next to Georgia. The nanny took up a position at the door, her chest heaving and her expression wrathful. "I have been dreadfully worried. We always breakfast together and his bed has not even been slept in."

"Have the police called here this morning, Miss Thorne?" Georgia asked gently, brushing the mussed curls back from the girl's face. She dreaded the moment when they must tell her, and watch the life fade from that heart-shaped little face.

"We sent for them last night, but they never came," Cora said. "Do you think they will come today?"

Georgia blinked at this unexpected information. "You sent for them? Last night?"

"Yes, after the man came in the window. Oh my goodness,

I was so frightened. I was waiting for the clock to strike midnight and then I told myself I would stop waiting for Papa and go to sleep. But I couldn't. Lucky thing, too, for the window opened and in he came."

Georgia glanced at Millie, whose face was turning pale. "What did you do?"

"Well, Papa and I play hide and seek all the time. So I simply rolled off the side of the bed against the wall, and hid under it."

Georgia fought off a sense of unreality while she asked, "You thought this was your papa?"

"Oh, no indeed. Just a burglar. And not a very good one. He didn't find me, and you know that under the bed is the first place one looks."

"Perhaps not when one is seeking jewels or money," Millie managed.

"He wouldn't have found either of those here," Cora said in a practical tone. "I overheard the nurse there tell the butler that there was no money for another month's stay. We will have to go home soon, I expect."

Thank goodness the nanny had not gone further and speculated about Sir Francis's risk-taking behavior, whatever that meant. There were things a child simply did not need to know.

But to the main point—why had a ruffian entered the child's room in the middle of the night? And was it connected to Sir Francis's death? Could the events have been simultaneous? Georgia pictured one man carrying off the child while another dispatched her father.

No, that couldn't have happened. For there had been no body on the water stairs when she and Millie had arrived home from the ball just after midnight. They had left Sir Francis at the Doge's palace alive and well, flinging glassware at the Conte di Narboni.

"So do you think they will come soon?" the child said. "The police?"

"Yes, I think so," Georgia said, collecting herself. "But before they do, there is something rather dreadful that we must tell you."

The girl went still, the way a rabbit will when a hawk glides overhead.

Georgia turned toward her on the sofa and took the girl's hands. "I am very much afraid that the reason the police are coming today is to inform you that your papa is dead."

Cora did not move. Her face paled to a dreadful almost-grey. "D-dead? Papa is dead?"

"Yes, darling. I found him upon our water stairs this morning."

"Your stairs?"

"Yes. He could have been coming to see us. To tell us something. Or perhaps it was only by chance. He seems to have fallen out of a gondola."

"Why didn't he come to *our* stairs?" The girl's face seemed to waver, and her eyes overflowed with the sudden tears of childhood ... or a woman's grief. "I waited and waited but he didn't come."

With a roar of desolation, the child flung herself into Georgia's arms. There was nothing Georgia could do but what she had done for darling Teddy—simply hold her, murmur soothing nothings, and wait until the poor child cried herself out.

"I want Mama," Cora croaked into Georgia's shoulder when she could get her breath.

"We will send for your mother at once, and the embassy will as well," Georgia said. "But in the meantime, until she arrives, would you like to stay with us at Villa dei Pappagalli?"

The child looked up, her face streaked with tears and misery. "Villa of the ... parrots?"

"Yes indeed. They are painted all over the walls. It is quite wonderful."

"Is there room for me?"

"Two rooms. You may choose between yellow parakeets and a rather terrifying green and blue macaw."

"P-parakeets, please."

A sensible choice. Millie had closed the door upon the macaw so they did not have to pass the angry thing every time they went to their rooms.

"Lovely. That is settled," Georgia said. "Is there a member of your household you would like with you? A governess or nanny?"

"No."

"You brought no staff with you from Bavaria?" Millie asked, fresh surprise in her tone. This was a diplomat's household, after all. "No one to take you out or give you lessons while your papa was busy with his work at the embassy?"

"No. We came by ourselves, in *Thetis*. She is a Zeppelin, since we live where they are made. It was supposed to be a grand adventure. And it was. Until—" Her face crumpled and she burrowed once more into Georgia's embrace.

I don't like the sound of this, Millie mouthed. Aloud, she said, "I will inform the nurse over there of our plans. She can tell

36

the police where we have gone. It should simplify things for them." She rose.

"You might also inform the staff that if their wages are paid to the end of the month, they may stay or not, as they please," Georgia said. "Cora will not be returning."

The nurse, informed of her employer's sudden passing, made no difficulty about packing up Cora's small traveling closet and her leather valise. Georgia had the impression that she would be glad to be shed of the child. The trunk was clearly brand new, and possessed very modern wheels on one side of its base so that it could be picked up by one handle and rolled rather than carried. Where, she asked herself, might such a wonder might be purchased?

Millie instructed the majordomo to send for the child's mother, and gave him one of her calling cards, on which she had written *Villa dei Pappagalli, San Polo*. "Lady Thorne may find her daughter here. Please reassure her the young lady will receive the best of care with us."

If Georgia was surprised that the staff made no effort to prevent the child going away with strangers, it was nothing to Lorenzo's surprise when at last he appeared to fetch them.

"Signorina Cora Thorne will be staying with us until her mother arrives from Bavaria," Georgia told him, as he eyed the girl and her luggage. "She is the daughter of the unfortunate man we discovered this morning."

"Ah, the poor little flower," he said, stowing her things, waiting for them to seat themselves, then maneuvering them out into the larger canal. "We will look after her."

"Did you happen to discover the owner of that gondola, Lorenzo?" Millie asked.

"I took it over to Paolo and he looked up the number."

"The gondolas are numbered?" Georgia said. How very organized. "We saw no such thing."

"On the keel," Lorenzo said. "You would not have seen it unless it was overturned."

"Who does it belong to?" Millie asked.

Likely the equivalent of a hansom driver.

"He does not know that—he only records who he sold it to. And that was Signore del Campo, in 1891."

"Del Campo," Millie repeated, all her attention on Lorenzo. "Is that a common name in Venice?"

Lorenzo laughed. "No, Signorina. There is only one family, among the first in the Duchy, and the most important member of it is the cabinet minister."

Millie's breath went out of her in a long exhale, though whether of discovery or horror, Georgia couldn't tell. "His name wouldn't be Arturo, would it?"

"*Si, Signorina.*" The gondola came within inches of scraping a building and with casual grace, Lorenzo pushed off it with his foot. "Paolo said he was very surprised when such an august personage ordered the construction of four plain gondolas. The other ones owned by the family, as you can imagine, are very grand, with cabins that can be closed with velvet curtains so the public may not gawk at the passengers. How did you know it was he, Signorina?"

"I didn't know about the gondolas," Millie said, sounding slightly winded. "But I danced with Arturo del Campo last night. I learned he is the minister in charge of public works for Venice."

"He is that," Lorenzo agreed. "But I would not advise you to dance with him again. He is a very dangerous man."

CHAPTER FOUR

*H*ow fortunate they were in the staff of the Villa dei Pappagalli! Georgia supposed that a boatman would mix with people from every neighborhood in Venice, and every level of society. If a young man were both observant and inclined to listen to those about him, he might pick up information about anyone from doge to dustman.

Public works, according to Lorenzo, was rather a misnomer. Millie's dance partner had his fingers in several pies, including the manufacture of the latest steam and hydraulic technologies, the operations of several of the builders' guilds, and a scheme that levied transfer taxes on airships landing at the Lido to take on water and coal and deliver the post. If an indignant captain refused to pay, the ship was seized and its crew thrown into prison until the money was humbly offered.

They had already learned the nature of a Venetian prison.

"I feel as though I have had a narrow escape," Millie confessed in an undertone as they disembarked at their little jetty and Lorenzo passed Cora's luggage up after the child.

"One is not accustomed to inquiring after the morals of one's partners in a ballroom," Georgia said as they went in.

Cora appeared to shake herself out of the torpor in which she had spent the journey, cuddled in Georgia's arms. "I could have told you not to dance with Signore del Campo, Miss Brunel," she said. "He has been to dinner at our house several times. I do not like him one bit."

"You dined with your father and the cabinet minister?" Millie asked in surprise.

"Oh, no. I listened under the window. The dining room looks out on the canal and the *fondamente*. I would simply sit under the casement enjoying the evening, and learn all manner of things."

It was clear they were going to have to keep a close eye on the girl. Though Georgia could hardly fault her for wanting to know what was going on. If no one thought of her amusement, she could not be blamed for making up her own.

Signore Airone met them in the receiving room, his brows rising at the sight of their guest. Georgia explained who Cora was, and that she would be staying in the parakeets' room until her mother arrived.

"Very well, my lady," he said. "But you have a guest waiting in the sitting room. A Signore Seacombe. May I inquire whether he will stay for lunch?"

Georgia opened her mouth to say no, then changed her mind. How had the man found them so quickly? And what errand would make it necessary to do so?

"*Si*, Signore," she said. "We will see him presently, once we have Signorina Thorne settled."

"I don't have to eat by myself, do I?" the girl asked plaintively, following Georgia and Millie up the stairs.

"Certainly not," Georgia said. "We are not so formal a household as that. And Mr. Seacombe, as you will discover, stands on no ceremony whatsoever. Just be careful of your toes."

They had only to remove their hats, and Georgia used her own brush to set Cora's unkempt curls in order, braiding it in two French plaits on either side of her head. "I always wanted a little girl," she said, assuaging the pain in her heart with the pleasure of looking after this fatherless child. "I warn you now, if I come home with frilly dresses for you, you are to order them sent back at once."

"I don't care much for frills, my lady," Cora said shyly. "But I would wear them if you wished me to. Until Mama comes. She will tell you she does not like them, either."

"We shall not risk it, then. There. You look very nice. Now we may all present ourselves to our guest without shame."

Dustin Seacombe looked very much as he had last night, except he might have changed his shirt. He took in Georgia's navy skirt and lacy middy blouse, then his gaze moved to Millie and Cora, missing nothing.

"Lady Langford. Miss Brunel. Miss Thorne," he said in his gravelly voice.

"How do you know my name?" Cora blurted even as she curtsied.

"The majordomo told me a minute ago," he said gravely. "But I saw you at the exhibition yesterday, too, with your father. My condolences on your loss. I did not know him, but he had a reputation as a kind and gallant man."

Cora's lips trembled, but she replied with the dignity of the bereaved, "Thank you, Mr. Seacombe."

41

Georgia indicated that they should move into the dining room, where lunch had been laid out. "News travels quickly."

"It depends on the kind of news," he said, holding a chair for her. "But I confess I was some way down the lane when I saw the monks come out your door bearing the—" He glanced at Cora, who had barely waited for her hostess to pick up her spoon before she tucked into her prawn and dumpling soup as though she had not had breakfast. "I have a friend at the monastery. He told me who had been brought in."

"We have been informed about the sad duties they perform before funerals," Millie said, sipping her own soup. "But perhaps we ought not to speak of such things, out of consideration for Cora's feelings."

Cora looked up, as though anyone's considering her feelings was a new sensation. "I don't mind. No one tells me anything. Not even the servants."

"There are some things it is better not to know, darling," Georgia said, unable to prevent the note of experience in her voice. "We will talk of other things."

And they did, until Georgia saw the child's appetite fade along with her energy, even before the main course. Her mouth drooped. In a moment the tears would overwhelm her.

"Come, Cora," she said gently. "A little sleep will do you good. The parakeets have promised to watch over you. No harm will come to you while in their care."

Tears were swimming in her eyes as she took Georgia's hand and they climbed the stairs to the third floor. "Even if a man comes?"

"Particularly then. Such a racket they would make."

Georgia suspected Cora was too old for such fancies, but in her grief, the picture of protective parakeets clearly appealed to her. She submitted to having her dress removed and being tucked into bed, and Georgia could not resist a kiss upon her forehead.

"You will not talk about anything interesting while I am asleep, will you?" Cora murmured.

Georgia made no promises. In fact, it occurred to her to wonder how long the child had been listening under windows, and how much she knew of her father's business.

"Rest now, little chick."

When she returned to the dining room, she discovered that the others had waited for her. "Now," she said, resuming her seat. "We may be frank with one another."

Mr Seacombe nodded. "If anything I say distresses you, I'll button my lip. My friend allowed me to watch the process with Sir Francis, and even to participate. I made several observations which you may or may not be interested in."

"I am interested," came out of Georgia's mouth before she could prevent it. But he, unlike the police, did not seem to think her a ghoul.

"It appeared to me that Sir Francis was struck with some force by a flat object," Mr Seacombe went on.

"Like the blade of an oar?" Millie asked. "We found one floating near the gondola."

"Possibly. The left side of his head was discolored by bruising, so I expect the blow was enough to send him into the water but not enough to kill him. He would have floated, not entirely conscious. He was subsequently held under by some means. There was a long bruise between his shoulder blades that indicates the oar, if that is what it was, may have been used for both purposes."

"How do you know he was held under?" Georgia asked, equal parts curious and horrified.

"Water in the lungs. The man was still breathing when he went in."

There was a clink as Millie's spoon dropped into her empty soup bowl. This was not Doctor Watson reporting on a case. This was someone they knew.

Mr Seacombe looked apologetic. "Sorry, ma'am. But these details help us understand what happened. And help us know who to look for."

Us? Was Mr Seacombe to participate in the matter in some way? Why should he do that? And what on earth had he been doing lurking about at the end of their lane this morning, Georgia wondered, if he had seen the monks bearing Sir Francis away?

"The monks will convey this information to the police?" Millie asked.

"Yes, ma'am. And a report will come to you, eventually. As the temporary guardians of his next of kin."

"We will be appropriately shocked when it does," Georgia said. "It will not be difficult."

The fish came in, swimming in a white wine sauce and surrounded by vegetables. As lunch was no formal affair, Georgia helped herself to the platter.

"You seem to know rather a lot about the, er, details, Mr Seacombe," Millie said, taking the platter from Georgia and serving herself. "How did you come by your knowledge? Are you a medical man?"

Their guest chuckled as he took his own portion of fish and vegetables. "No indeed, ma'am. I'm a Texican Ranger."

His companions gazed at him blankly.

"I see I'll have to explain." He put down the platter, then went on, "I'm from the Texican Territories, as I told Lady Langford last night. I'm a member of a widely scattered policing force there. We have detachments in settled places like Denver, Santa Fe, and Texico City, and in not so settled places, too. The outfit has its problems, but most of us are proud of the work we do."

Georgia opened her mouth to ask how that work had brought him to Venice, then changed her mind. He hadn't answered her last night; it wasn't likely he would do so this morning, guest or not.

"I'd like a look at that gondola, with your permission."

"We have learned it was purchased by Arturo del Campo four years ago," Georgia said, feeling rather pleased that she, too, had facts to dispense.

His fork paused in midair. "You don't say."

She wanted to be flippant, but it didn't seem right. Not with Cora asleep upstairs.

"Gondolas are numbered," Millie said before she could speak.

"I didn't know that," he said.

"The young man who acts as our gondolier went to inquire of the gondola maker near the Accademia this morning and was given that information," Millie explained. "However, while Signore del Campo may have ordered the vessel made, it does not follow that four years later he still owns it. Someone else may well do so now, putting us right back where we began."

"Might be able to find that out," Mr Seacombe mused. "And you said an oar was found nearby?"

"Yes," Georgia said. "I'm afraid I used it to bring the

gondola in closer so we could secure it. I hope I did not cause any damage to the … evidence."

"If it's been in the water awhile, likely not. I'd still like a look."

"After lunch," Georgia said firmly, and steered the conversation into calmer waters. "Are you by chance any relation of the Seacombes of the Seacombe Steamship Company in England?"

His gaze kindled into a glare. "Now what would make you say that?"

Dear me. So much for calmer waters. But she did not apologize, nor hurry the topic away. This was her table, after all. And he owed her for her abused toes. "It is not so common a name."

"Are you acquainted with that family?"

"No indeed, though my son is—with Claude, I believe his name is. Rather a raffish young man but quite harmless. He visited once during a school holiday."

"Small world."

"Indeed."

Silence fell. Georgia waited, while Millie looked between them, clearly sensing the tension in the air.

At last Mr Seacombe sighed. "If you know the boy, I s'pose I might as well 'fess up. He'd be a cousin of some sort, I guess. His grandparents are my aunt and uncle."

"Is that Howel Seacombe? Were you aware he had passed?" Millie asked. "I only inquire because of your use of the present tense."

"Is that so?" A frown came and went under the wavy brown hair disheveled by the removal of his Stetson hat. "Don't remember much of him. My father was his youngest brother. The two of them got into a ruckus years ago and never spoke again. Dad took the family to the Fifteen Colonies when I was just a boy."

Their guest must be in his middle forties now, if the grey salting his temples and moustache was any indication. "Are your parents still living?" Georgia asked.

He shook his head. "Flash flood got 'em both while we were crossing the badlands. Had to live by my wits until I could hop a train to Santa Fe. A woman there took me in. She kept a boarding-house. Still does. I did odd jobs for my keep. Joined the Rangers soon as I was old enough."

Georgia was silent, taking in the enormity of a picture outlined in so few words. She had lost her mother, too, but not until she was a woman grown. To be a child in a strange country and lose both parents under such terrible circumstances? What *was* a flash flood, if it could kill? She had never heard of such a thing before this moment, but she was certain she would not forget it.

"I am sorry you suffered such a loss so young," Millie said quietly, and reached across the corner of the table to lay a hand upon his, which was clenched around his fork.

Deliberately, he relaxed his fingers, released the fork to turn over his hand, and squeezed hers. "Thank you, ma'am. The loss does get smaller over time. It never really leaves you. But it gets small enough to live with."

Georgia realized she had just seen the birth of a friendship. What a quartet they were in this villa—two without parents, two with only one remaining. Perhaps she would write to Papa when she wrote to Teddy this afternoon, and tell him of Venice. Its warm skies and waterways were as different from the rolling hills and granite outcrops of home as rum sauce was from mutton. He would enjoy hearing of it, even if he could not imagine it. Perhaps she ought to buy some postcards and enclose them so that he could see what she described.

"And what of your nearer family, Mr Seacombe?" Millie asked. "Do you have a wife and children waiting upon your return from Venice?"

The corner of his mouth lifted, and he flicked a brief glance at Georgia before politely replying, "No, ma'am. Never been married. Never had the time for courting."

Georgia sat as though pinned to her chair. In a single glance, in half a smile, he had told her, *I'm interested. I wonder if you are, too.*

Good heavens above.

No, indeed she was not.

This untidy, rude person! This Texican!

Unthinkable.

Which meant she would now be unable to *not* think about it.

Fool! Was she mad?

Never again.

Never. Ever. Again.

GEORGIA, Millie noticed, was unusually silent for the remainder of luncheon. Millie did her best to direct the conversation from topic to topic, as a good hostess might, in search of common ground.

Afterward, Millie was relieved to move outside to the water stairs so that Mr Seacombe could examine the gondola.

The vessel was too heavy even for him to turn over to see the number on the keel. Lorenzo was happy to give it to him, however—as well as the numbers of the other three vessels in the cabinet minister's order.

Could she really have danced with a man who could kill?

But no, that was unjust. A cabinet minister did not steer English diplomats about the canals of the city. He would hire a gondolier to do so. Who would then be the one to kill him.

If he still owned the vessel. What was the likelihood of that? Goodness, what a suspicious person she was becoming! The cabinet minister might be a perfectly pleasant man, despite what a ten-year-old thought of him. He had certainly been so during their dance. Why should anyone suspect him of such a crime?

Had they been in England, and Sir Francis had been pushed off a steamship, or a punt, or a sailboat, it would have been different. There were bills of sale exchanged between owner and buyer. Records kept. Presumably one could find the owner, determine if there had been a quarrel, and inquire from there. But who knew what the Duchy could supply in the way of continuity and helpful documents?

Honestly, if Mr Seacombe wanted to discover who had killed Sir Francis, he had a job of work ahead of him. Though why it should involve him was a mystery. This was a matter for the Duchy police, or the embassy, not foreigners like themselves.

Leaving the gondola to float undisturbed on its tether once more, the Ranger's attention turned to the oar. He examined the blade minutely, to the extent of pulling something like a very short telescope, or half a pair of opera glasses, from the pocket of his waistcoat.

"Hm," he grunted, peering into it.

"Yes?" Georgia asked, speaking for the first time in several minutes.

"Look here." He tilted the oar in her direction, the instrument poised above one edge. "It's cracked."

She did so, then said, "Is that ... a thread?"

"More likely a hair."

He invited Millie to look through the brass instrument. She saw instantly that it was indeed a hair of about two inches in length, caught in the crack as though it were a vise. "Brown, like that of Sir Francis," she observed. "Do you suppose that crack was made when it collided with the poor man?"

"Mr Seacombe, this oar must indeed be the murder weapon. You were not merely speculating earlier." Georgia said. While it was clear to Millie she was doing her best not to be missish, her face had gone a little pale.

"It was a possibility. Now maybe it's more."

"Then we ought to turn it over to the police," Millie said. When he did not respond, only continued to examine the blade minutely with the ocular instrument, she and Georgia exchanged a glance. "Oughtn't we?"

"Let's see their report first," he said easily, pocketing the instrument and raising the oar to resting position. "Do you have a safe place to keep this?"

Define safe, Millie was tempted to say.

"Will an empty closet do?" Georgia asked. "In the macaw's room. No one in their right mind would go in there."

"An excellent suggestion," Millie said. "Ah, here is Signore Airone to show Mr Seacombe the way." They left together, and Millie seized her opportunity. "Are you all right, dear?"

"Yes, of course."

Hmph. The standard reply. "You seemed very quiet after Mr Seacombe revealed his marital status."

Georgia glared at her. "What has that to do with anything? A man has been murdered on our doorstep, and I handled the murder weapon myself. Anyone would be horrified at contemplating such a thing."

So. Dustin Seacombe's marital status mattered. Good heavens. How very unexpected.

"Of course they would," Millie said soothingly. "I shall be interested in that policeman's report. Did it strike you that Mr Seacombe doesn't seem to believe it will contain the facts as we know them?"

Georgia took a deep breath and when she spoke, her tone was more moderate. "I observed one or two hints in that direction. I wonder how much experience he has with the Duchy police? And how exactly does one acquire a friend in a monastery?"

"I do not know, but I can assert with ninety-nine percent probability that he will never tell us."

CHAPTER FIVE

ith a child in the house, the shape of their days was forced to change. Any inclination Georgia might have had to laziness, to drinking cappucino as she whiled away a morning painting the new views at hand, vanished. It now fell to them to keep Cora's mind occupied with new sights, and since they had intended to see them anyway, they simply attended to their itinerary with more energy.

One had to do something to help the poor child. And while there were still tears, Georgia had not forgotten the knack of comfort, or of the medicinal benefits of hugs and cuddles to a girl coming to grips with the sudden absence of a beloved father and a mother whose arrival was looked for at every moment.

So, on Thursday, the day after Cora had come to them, they took a public steamboat out to observe the glass blowers on the island of Burano. On Friday, they visited Murano, the island of lace makers.

Murano, it turned out, was as close as a woman of fashion could get to heaven.

Georgia immediately became the proud possessor of a three-foot lace square so intricately wrought one could only see the beauty of the patterns, not distinguish individual loops and stitches. It would look very fine on the table in the hall of the town house, under a vase of fresh flowers. She bought three lacy collars in different neckline shapes to trim dresses with, and secretly, a box of lace-trimmed handkerchiefs to give to Millie at Christmas.

She hadn't been this happy in months, she thought, as she carried off her purchases in triumph.

That afternoon they visited Santa Maria del Saluté, which had been built to thank the Lady of Heaven for sending the plague from the city. It was very lovely, but it soon became apparent that admiring churches was not the best thing to do with an child like Cora, who was torn between the urge to run and the need to cry at the sight of people praying. As for the Isola di San Michele, the cemetery island—well, it was simply out of the question.

Saturday, May 4, 1895

"I am beginning to wonder if anyone has sent for Lady Thorne at all," Millie murmured as they crossed the Grand Canal in a graceful little steam vessel called a *vaporetto*. "She ought to have been here by now. Bavaria is a flight of only a few hours over the Alps."

"I was thinking that myself," Georgia replied. Cora was on the other side of the vessel, leaning out to see where they were going, and the engine was noisy, so she could not possibly hear. But still. "She ought to have been here yesterday, even had the message been sent on a slow airship carrying freight. Which of course it could not have been—surely they would have sent someone in person. I have been thinking over what we ought to do."

"Return to London?" Millie suggested.

"No, not yet. But I do think we ought to call at the embassy, to see if they have heard any particulars of Lady Thorne's arrival."

There was no time like the present.

It was not difficult to find the English embassy—it was across the square from the Doge's palace, as were those of several other countries, including the Fifteen Colonies. The young English gentleman in the reception office looked mystified at their inquiry.

"Lady Thorne? Do you mean to say she has not yet arrived?"

Oh dear. Georgia took Cora's hand to give it a reassuring squeeze. "No. Sir Francis died sometime in the early hours of the first of May. The police told us later that morning that they would contact you that same day, to notify her."

"They did so, and we sent a letter by diplomatic packet, Lady Langford," the gentleman said. "Protocol must be followed in cases such as this."

"Of course." Georgia did not point out that protocol was not producing the desired result.

"Terribly sad," the man said with a sigh. "Sir Francis was well liked here. But Venice is a tricky place for the unaware."

"What do you mean?" Millie asked. She took Cora's other hand.

He made an expansive gesture that encompassed the

square outside, and the palace standing opposite. "Politics, of course. Factions fighting one another and attempting to draw in representatives of other countries for support. Sir Francis spent entire days trying to keep the Minister of Public Works from throttling the Minister of Transportation, and vice versa. And then it would all blow over and they would share a glass of brandy together as if nothing had happened."

"Goodness," Millie managed.

"That sounds like Papa," Cora said in a small voice, as though she was not certain she was permitted to speak in her late father's place of employment.

The young man smiled over the desk at her. "He had a good relationship with Minister del Campo. Though for my part, I often thought he had to draw upon all his reserves of good breeding to deal with him. Del Campo is feared more than he is liked, and yet, it is vital that the relationship between the Venetian government and Her Majesty remains cordial. For it is certainly profitable."

"Oh?" Georgia said. "In what way?"

But he had already moved on to further definitions of *tricky*. "And then there are the bridges, and this gearworks business. You'd think someone would have thought to stop the blessed city from revolving, so that a man could get from one place to another without a compass and telescope. To say nothing of the canals themselves."

"Do they carry disease?" Millie asked, a note of anxiety in her tone.

"No, thank goodness, but they cannot be said to be pristine as a Scottish loch, can they? And one is always having to hire a gondolier, never quite certain one is not being cheated. What a way to meet one's demise. Drowning in a canal." He shuddered, clearly having quite forgotten a bereaved child was standing in front of him.

"Please do not speak that way of Sir Francis," Georgia said. How did this man know how he had died? Was it common knowledge? And if so, why had they not been told the verdict was in?

"I beg your pardon, ladies. Yes, we received the police report this morning. For of course Her Majesty will have to be informed, so that another diplomat may be appointed to the post."

"Would it be possible to see the report?" Georgia was undecided how to approach this. With the imperiousness of her ladyship, or the concern of a temporary mother? The man was young, so she decided on the latter. "As you see, this is Sir Francis's daughter Cora. She is staying with us until her mother arrives. While of course I would never share details outside we four, her family does deserve to know the contents of that report. Don't you agree?"

She put as much pleading into her gaze as she could.

He folded like a napkin. "Of course, your ladyship. One moment, and I will fetch it."

When he laid the single sheet of paper before them, it took Georgia a moment to decipher the crabbed handwriting. What there was of it. She was not in the habit of reading reports of people's deaths outside of *The Times*, but surely there had to be more to a police investigation than this?

"Millie, will you translate?" she asked, spotting the name of their villa at the bottom of a brief paragraph, following particulars of names and dates.

"Certainly. *Between the hours of midnight and eight of the clock, the victim fell into a canal near the Villa dei Pappagalli and drowned. No witnesses were found. The individual who discovered the body reported it timely. She was also one of the last people to see the victim alive. Further questioning warranted."*

Georgia raised her eyes to the young man. "What does that mean, sir?"

"I do not know," he said. "Is it a concern?"

"It certainly is, since I am the *individual* in the case."

"You, Lady Langford?" His eyebrows rose halfway to his unfortunately receding hairline. "How is that possible?"

Before he got completely the wrong idea, Georgia said, "My last dance at the king and queen's ball on the thirtieth was with Sir Francis. When I left, he was still in the ballroom, having words with the Conte di Narboni. There is no *coincidence*, other than his fetching up on our water stairs. Am I really to be subjected to the questioning of those policemen a second time?"

"Certainly not," he said in soothing tones, though she could not fathom how he could give such an assurance. He had no authority to order policemen about. "Would you like to speak to the ambassador about it?"

"No," she said reluctantly. "I will not trouble him with coincidence and speculation. My greater concern is that Lady Thorne is duly notified of her husband's death. For Cora's sake, I wish to be assured that she is on her way."

"We will contact the booking office and notify you as soon as we have her arrival time."

"Thank you." She gave him her card and her most winning smile, and then there was nothing else to do but return to the villa. They had to disembark from the vaporetto at the nearest public pier and walk the last hundred yards, for Lorenzo had not been with them today.

"Lady Langford?" Cora said as they entered the house.

"Yes, darling. Would you like some refreshment? Some lemonade?"

"Yes, please. Do you know why that report says nothing about the number on the gondola, or where it is, or the oar, or anything?"

Georgia led the way upstairs into the sunny sitting room on the floor above, and collapsed upon the sofa. She unpinned her hat as she spoke. "That, my dear, is the question that has been plaguing my mind like a mosquito all the way home. And how, might I ask, do you know about the oar?"

The girl blushed, and sat upon the edge of the sofa, as if she thought Georgia might brush her off like a piece of lint. "I did not fall asleep right away the other day. The windows were open."

Georgia did not like to think of the graphic details the child had heard. "I am sorry if we upset you by our conversation. I would have prevented it had I known."

"Mama says that when I am a spy, sometimes I will not like what I hear."

"Your mama is quite right. Come here, child. I am quite in need of a hug after all this."

After Cora had obliged her, and Georgia had kissed the top of her head, she snuggled into her side.

"Now I understand why Mr Seacombe seemed to think the report would not reflect the facts," Millie said, laying her own hat aside. "But I would very much like to know why he thought so. And why they do not."

"And I should like to know if I am to expect another visit from the Long and the Short of it," Georgia said, then brightened as she caught sight of their majordomo. "Ah, Signore Airone. You are a treasure."

He laid out refreshments on a low table between the sofas, and poured glasses of cool lemonade. When they had biscuits and cake as well, he said, "A telegram came for you, Signora."

"Goodness me. Already?"

But it was not the arrival time of Lady Thorne's vessel she found on the yellow paper.

To: Lady Langford, Villa Dei Pappagalli, Venice

From: D. Brucker, Kastanienhof, Munich

Lady Thorne not in residence Stop Whereabouts not divulged to staff Stop Will convey message upon return Stop Condolences to Miss Thorne End

"Who or what is Kastanienhof?" Georgia wondered aloud, mystified. "Cora, is that the name of your house?" She handed her the telegram, and Millie read it over her shoulder.

"Yes," the girl said. "It's called that because of the chestnut trees along the avenue. And Herr Brucker is our Signore Airone. But it makes no sense. Mama was working on a terribly important project for the Empress. Other than dashing over here to fetch me, she would never leave her laboratory."

But if she was not on her way to Venice, where was she? And how had she been informed of her husband's death if she was not there? "Do you suppose she is on her way?"

"Not without telling Herr Brucker where she was going." Cora was firm about that.

59

"Unless it was a surprise," Millie suggested, with the air of someone clinging to hope in the face of disaster.

Cora gazed at her a moment. "You haven't met my mother. She plans things down to the phase of the moon and which way the wind is blowing. Mama does not enjoy surprises."

"Goodness me." Georgia felt quite justified in taking another piece of cake. "I am glad we brought all your things with us, darling. We will look after you, and shall be a cozy household of three until she arrives."

"But she will come, won't she?" Georgia's heart broke at the fear in Cora's eyes at the thought of another parent being taken from her.

"Your mama, from what you have said, is a woman of immense resources," Georgia said with a firmness she did not feel. "If I were she, nothing on earth could prevent me from coming for you. I think we may have complete confidence in her."

She could only hope she was right.

LATER IN THE AFTERNOON, a note came on thick, creamy paper from the ambassador himself.

Dear Lady Langford,

I regret that I was not informed of your visit earlier today. It is unconscionable that Sir Francis's family and friends were left standing in the vestibule, and not shown every courtesy and sympathetic hospitality of which Her Majesty's representative in the Duchy is capable. Said functionary, you may be sure, has been disciplined and educated upon the subject.

I beg the honor of waiting upon you at the Villa dei Pappagalli at four of the clock today. I have information to convey that will interest you, and wish to return the few personal mementoes Sir Francis kept about him.

Yours faithfully,

Maj. Gen. Ernest Davies-Howe, KBE

Envoy to the Duchy of Venice by appointment of the Queen

Georgia glanced in some dismay at the porcelain clock upon the mantel. It was three fifteen.

"Dear me, I suppose we must change into tea gowns. How very inconvenient."

"Why should we change?" Cora asked. "We would have been wearing these very clothes if we had been admitted to his office earlier."

Georgia admired the logic of the child's mind, and regretted having to say, "While you are quite right, when one is notified in writing of a knight's coming to call, one displays equal courtesy in appearing in clothes appropriate not only for the guest, but also for the time of day."

"Clothes go by the hour?" Cora asked, puzzled. "Mine don't."

"That is because of your tender years, darling," Millie said. "For ladies of ours, it is morning gowns, walking costumes, tea gowns, dinner gowns, and evening dress if one is going out."

"My word. Mama doesn't have any of those things, only skirts and blouses and a leather apron for the laboratory. Well," she amended, "I suppose she does have an evening gown. And a tiara. It was a wedding present from Papa."

"A lovely and appropriate gift." Georgia's own sapphire

tiara and parure were in the safe, and had also been a wedding gift. Hartford had been a man of good taste … and distasteful habits. She rose and held out her hand. "But Miss Brunel is quite right. Tea gowns it is. On the bright side, we will be able to enjoy another helping of cake and biscuits when he comes."

Major General Sir Ernest Davies-Howe arrived on the tick of the dot at the water stairs, and was shown up to the sitting room, where he bowed over Georgia's hand. Millie and Cora curtsied, and the former, as the eldest lady, poured tea.

Georgia had seen many a man like this—brusque and impatient behind a handlebar moustache and glossy boots. She had not seen so many capable of such kindness as he showed Cora. The child seemed to have a gift for making people like her. Or perhaps it was her sad situation that touched their hearts. In any case, once profuse apologies for their treatment at the embassy were out of the way, Sir Ernest helped her to cake as though she were his own daughter.

"You said in your note, Sir Ernest, that you had information for us," Georgia said, enjoying her tea. "If it was the police report of Sir Francis's death, do not trouble yourself. We have seen it."

"I know, dear lady," he said, sieving his tea through his moustache, then wiping his mouth with a snowy napkin. "I came rather to discuss with you the details of his funeral. Now that his remains have been released by the monks, we can have the service at San Giuseppe d'Arimatea—the English church, don't you know, not far from here—and then the coffin can be sent home to England."

"To England?" Millie said, surprised.

"But we live in Munich," Cora told him. "We have since I was born."

"Yes, I know." Sir Ernest nodded. "But I am sure he did not plan to stay there the rest of his life. He would have returned to his estate in his retirement, like the rest of us, hey?"

"I do not know of any estate," Cora said uncertainly. "I only know Kastanienhof."

"Then such decisions may be made by your mother, once she arrives. Which I devoutly hope is soon. Because of the climate, you understand, the funeral can be no later than Tuesday. Will eleven o'clock suit? And a luncheon at the embassy afterward?"

Goodness. Would Lady Thorne even be here by Tuesday? On the other hand, a funeral could not be postponed indefinitely.

"Will that be all right, darling?" she asked Cora.

"I ... suppose so. But what if Mama does not come in time?"

Georgia thought quickly. "Then you will represent the family as principal mourner, and Aunt Millie and I will support you. You must remember to take a rose from the bouquet, and press it for your mother as a memento."

The thought of a concrete task she could perform for her mother seemed to give her something to cling to. "Yes. All right."

"I had thought you might prefer it were held here," the ambassador confided to Georgia, "but my wife assured me that you should not be burdened with the need to host such an event when the young lady is in mourning."

It had not occurred to Georgia to prefer to do any such thing. In her calculations, there had only been Lady Thorne and a return home for Cora, with or without her husband's coffin.

"Thank you for your kind consideration, Sir Ernest, and for seeing to all the arrangements," she murmured.

He leaned down and opened the satchel he had brought in with him. "Here are Sir Francis's effects." He laid them on the table beside the tea things.

An appointment diary. A corkscrew. A cambric handkerchief, laundered. And a daguerreotype of himself standing with his family before a painted screen featuring a jewelbox of a house that seemed to be made of white marble, framed by trees.

"Our picture," Cora said. She picked it up and tilted it toward Georgia. "I have one, too, next to my bed. We had the likeness taken while the Empress's fancy for making daguerreotypes lasted. That behind us is a tapestry of Linderhof, the royal palace where she was born, and where her laboratory is."

Georgia took the framed picture and studied it. She had no interest in palaces, but she was interested in Lady Thorne. Cora's mother gazed back in the solemn, immobile fashion of daguerreotypes, dressed in a traveling suit of what appeared to be wool gabardine, her blouse with a crystal-pleated stand-up white collar nearly to her chin. Her hair was piled under a low-crowned top hat, its veil trailing over her shoulder and a pair of goggles pushed up on the brim to keep the wind from her eyes. She was as tall as Sir Francis, with winged brows, dark eyes sparkling with intelligence, and a chin of such authority it must have struck fear in the hearts of her staff.

"Your mother is a fine-looking woman," she said to Cora, handing the picture to Millie. "But that signifies nothing next to her obvious intelligence and determination, visible even in a daguerreotype."

Cora beamed up at her. "I think so, too. She says I will be like her someday, but I cannot see it."

There were the winged eyebrows and the intelligence. The chin had been softened by her father's contribution to her biology, but its authority could still be traced.

"I can," Georgia assured her, then turned her smile upon Sir Ernest. "Thank you for bringing these to Cora, Sir Ernest. It was kind of you."

"The least I could do," he said, and rose. "Thank you for permitting me to call."

She escorted him to the sitting-room door so that Signore Airone could see him out, where he paused. "One more thing, Lady Langford."

"Yes?"

"If Lady Thorne doesn't turn up, what will become of Cora? For you cannot be expected to play nursemaid indefinitely."

"No indeed. But we are happy she has joined our little party. She is a delightful and intelligent child." That said, Georgia had already turned the question over in her mind in the quiet watches of the night. "We cannot very well take her back to England with us without further knowledge of her family and connections. So if needs must, we will set our course for Munich, where hopefully her mother will have returned from her errand and be glad and relieved to welcome her."

With a nod, he clicked his boot heels together and bowed. "Until Tuesday, then."

She inclined her head, and Signore Airone showed him down the stairs and back to his waiting gondolier.

Georgia returned to the sofa and picked up her teacup, but did not drink.

Cora put the picture on the table, her fingers caressing her mother's upright form. "Mama will turn up. You'll see."

"What good ears you have, darling."

"I know. She says I have the ears and eyes of a spy, not the hands of an inventor like her." She paged through the appointment diary, her attention distracted by her father's handwriting and evidence of an official life she had not been privy to.

Over the girl's head, Georgia's gaze met Millie's. The ambassador had asked a reasonable question. What indeed would they do if Lady Thorne had met the same fate as her husband, at the hands of persons unknown? What if her daughter were already an orphan?

CHAPTER SIX

*S*ignore Airone had barely cleared away the tea trays and returned to his normal duties when the bell on the street side of the villa rang. He had an air of long-suffering patience as he appeared once more in the doorway of the sitting room.

"La polizia, Signora. Di nuovo."

Again was right. For here came the Long and the Short of it, looking even more baleful and suspicious than they had on their first visit. Georgia took her seat on the sofa beside Millie, and bade them sit on the opposite sofa.

They declined. What a lucky thing that Cora had taken her father's belongings upstairs. Georgia wanted a look at that appointment diary, and she'd be dashed if she'd hand it over to these two, only to have it as conveniently misplaced as the facts of Sir Francis's death.

"Are you here to deliver your report of the unfortunate death of Sir Francis Thorne?" she asked politely. Her mother-in-law, who had never liked her, would have said she was being a troublemaker.

She would have been right.

Once again, Millie obliged with a translation.

"No, Signora," Long said. "But we will convey our conclusions—that Sir Francis Thorne fell from his gondola and drowned."

"I see." It was difficult not to appear skeptical at this bland statement of the obvious. Besides, how he might have done that if he were seated in it, as everyone was until they got to the place where they were to disembark? Gondolas did not just overturn as though they were coracles.

"Have you anything to tell us about what happened, Signora?" Millie's voice faltered on the translation, and she cleared her throat.

Puzzled, Georgia gazed at Short, who had asked the question. "I'm afraid not. I was sleeping and heard nothing, not even a splash."

"Then how do you account for his floating at your water stairs?"

"I cannot. But since we read your report while at the English embassy, why don't we cease dancing about, and get to the real reason you are here."

They looked at one another, and Georgia felt rather maliciously pleased. Nothing like rolling the big guns out on the hilltop, as her grandfather used to say.

"The ambassador himself just called upon us," Millie added pleasantly.

These two ought to know that they were not simply defenseless tourists. They were gentlewomen with social connections in this city, and what's more, knew how to use them.

"Your report appears to draw a connection between my dancing with Sir Francis at Their Majesties' ball on Tuesday, and his appearance in the canal outside sometime Wednesday morning," Georgia said crisply. "Since Miss Brunel and I left at midnight and Sir Francis was still breathing—rather heavily, I should imagine, since he was shouting at the Conte di Narboni at the time—then I fail to see how the two events can be related."

"I do not believe in coincidence, Signora," Short said. "Not in a crime of this nature."

Georgia pounced. "So you have concluded it is a crime, and not an accident, then?"

But he was a match for her. "*Sì*, Signora. A man does not steer himself to a woman's home and fall out of his gondola before he has seen the woman."

The nerve of him!

Millie could contain herself no longer. "Are you implying Lady Langford had an—an *assignation* with Sir Francis? How dare you!" Then she had to translate her own question for Georgia.

"If not an assignation, then certainly a lovers' quarrel," Short went on while Georgia's blood pressure climbed another notch. "The signora might have met him on the water stairs, and pushed him into the canal in anger. The facts lend themselves to such a view, you must admit."

"I admit no such thing," Georgia snapped. "I neither arrange liaisons nor quarrel with married men. I had no connection with Sir Francis Thorne except for one meeting with my husband three years ago in England, and Tuesday at the exhibition and the ball, accompanied at all times by Signorina Brunel, my husband's aunt, whom you see. There is nothing more, and I resent your impugning my character in suggesting there is!"

Short gave a surprisingly graceful bow. "Our apologies, Signora, but we must follow every avenue of investigation open to us."

Georgia closed her teeth on the hot words that would have contradicted him, for the proof he was lying was at this moment upstairs under the macaw's watchful painted eye. They had concealed evidence at the request of Dustin Seacombe, and now she, at least, was having second thoughts about it. How dared the Texican place them in such a position!

"Of course you must," she said, controlling her temper with an effort. "I hope I have assisted sufficiently."

"You have assisted," he allowed. "What are your immediate plans, Signora?"

What did he mean? What business was it of his? "We are tourists," Millie said slowly, watching them. "We plan to see the sights of Venice. And to paint *en plein air.*"

"And when that is concluded?"

"We have not decided," Georgia said when Millie had translated. She would omit any mention of Lady Thorne and her puzzling failure to appear at such a difficult time in her daughter's young life.

"Allow me to assist you in the decision, then," Long said smoothly. "Please do not leave Venice until you are informed you may go."

"I beg your pardon?" Surely she must have misheard.

He repeated it. A veritable storm of words poured out of Millie, which she afterward recounted to Georgia. She tore a strip off the two policemen, asserting that they had no right to detain two English women of noble family who were clearly innocent, no matter what state their investigation was in.

But the Long and the Short of it were unmoved.

Short bowed again. "Good afternoon, Signora. Signorina. Thank you for your time."

Signore Airone led them away at a march, his back stiff with offense.

Georgia rather had her back up, too. "How dare they!"

"My sentiments exactly," Millie said. "The nerve! As if a woman so recently out of mourning is going to have *assignations* with men she hardly knows—with or without a quarrel."

Georgia said, "I shall report this visit to the ambassador when we see him at church. For how long, pray, are we to wait for their investigation to wind to its conclusion?"

Millie raised an eyebrow. Then together they exhaled and said, "It's Italy."

Sunday, May 5, 1895

On Sundays, it seemed, all of the Duchy devoted itself to church and family, no matter how many of the commandments had been broken the night before. Georgia, Millie, and Cora attended the English church service at San Giuseppe d'Arimatea, near the embassy, on the information of Signore Airone. The man was a treasure. What he didn't know about his city could fit in a thimble, with room left over.

Since the funeral would be held there on Tuesday, it was no surprise to discover the ambassador himself in attendance. As they shook hands outside afterward, Georgia quietly unburdened herself on the subject of the visit from the *polizia* the day before.

"The nerve of them!" he exclaimed.

"Exactly what we said."

"I have a good relationship with the chief man. Leave it with me, Lady Langford. We can't very well have a baron's mother scrubbing gears underwater, can we?"

"Certainly not," Georgia said, appalled at the image. "Thank you, Sir Ernest."

Georgia then declined an invitation to lunch, citing their need to get Cora home in case there was news of her mother. No matter how elegant the meal might have been on the top floor of the embassy, it couldn't have been as good as the lunch of pasta with shrimp and vegetables that Signore Airone produced with a flourish, nor the *secondi* of a roasted cutlet with rosemary sauce that followed.

"Now," Georgia said, so full that she rose from the table rather less gracefully than an airship rose from its landing field, "Cora, if you do not mind, I should very much like a look at your father's appointment diary. Would that be all right?"

"Of course, Auntie Georgia. There isn't anything very interesting in it, but I'll fetch it."

They had decided that the three of them should be on more informal terms. Millie rather liked being auntie to another intelligent, lovable child. For her part, Georgia missed Teddy dreadfully. She refused to consider how empty the town house would seem when they returned to London.

"A good idea, dear," Millie said as the child clattered up the stairs. "Unlike the police, we shall leave no stone unturned."

"And then we must go for a walk. I am so full my corset ribbons are creaking in an ominous fashion."

"Perhaps we might request that the kitchen confine itself to one course," Millie suggested.

"They would probably resign on the spot. For my part, I would do better simply to eat less."

Better, but unsatisfying, when it all tasted so good.

Cora returned with the diary, and sat between them on the sitting-room sofa to turn the pages while they looked it over. "Where shall we begin? January?"

"We may return there if we need to," Millie said. "But it seems to me the beginning of April would be most useful."

The diary was of the sort with the month named at the top, a week on each spread, and a generous space for each day's appointments. Across the bottom of each page was engraved EMBASSY OF HER MAJESTY VICTORIA REGINA.

It didn't specify which embassy, so all of them could be supplied more cheaply, one supposed. Georgia wrestled her thoughts into order and concentrated on the entries.

April 3—EDH lunch. And each Friday thereafter.

"A standing appointment with Sir Ernest was to be expected," Georgia said. "Sir Francis did report to him."

April 16—ADC 4:00.

Millie leaned in. "Arturo del Campo? How maddening of your papa to only use initials, Cora. Was he distrustful of observers in the embassy, I wonder, or merely short of time?"

"Short of time, probably," Cora said, hunting for more appearances of those initials. "Papa and the clock did not get along. He always said he'd be late for his own—" She stopped.

Funeral, as the saying went.

Georgia squeezed her shoulders and redirected her attention. "If that does indeed stand for del Campo, he seems to have met with him twice at the embassy, and then look." She pointed to a scribble in the margin.

April 18—Doge—ADC/ADN 8:00.

"Doge's palace, del Campo and someone else, for dinner?" Millie guessed. "There's another, two nights later, same people, only it says *Delf*. What is that, I wonder? A restaurant?"

"No indeed," Cora said. "That is our house. Villa dei Delfini."

"House of the Dolphins," Millie translated for Georgia. "How lovely."

"Not really," Cora said, turning pages for more instances of *ADC/ADN*. "At low tide, you can smell the drains."

Oh dear.

"Cora," Georgia said suddenly, "what is the name of the transportation minister, do you know?"

"Alessandro di Narbone—oh! Of course. I'm so sorry, what a dunce I am! Papa has been meeting with them quite a lot lately. At home and other places. When I told you I listened under the window, that was here." She flipped two pages and rested a finger under the notation.

Delf—ADC/ADN 9:00.

"Is Alessandro a relation of the Conte di Narboni?"

"A cousin, I think. Everybody in politics here is related, it seems to me," the girl said.

"What were they talking of, do you remember? You said you learned all manner of things."

"Airships was one of the things. About the transfer tax. Terribly dull. Except for when they started to argue about it. Then it got interesting—they broke a plate banging a fist down on it."

"Goodness," Georgia said. "Interesting, indeed."

"I nearly fell in the canal from fright. And trains. They don't come here, you know. They stop on the mainland and then one takes a steamboat across. But Signore di Narbone was keen to build a bridge over the lagoon. He can't, of course."

"Because of the gearworks," Millie said, nodding. "One can hardly build a train station if one cannot depend on its being there when the train arrives."

"Exactly," Cora agreed. "Let's see, what else did they talk about? Ladies, but I covered my ears. Signore del Campo's mother-in-law. I learned a lot of swear words that night. Italian ones. Mostly they spoke English for Papa, but the swearing was in Italian."

Millie closed her eyes briefly, as though in pain.

"Oh, and a breakwater. They were talking about that just before we met you." She flipped to the page. "See?"

April 29—Delf—ADC/ADN 11:00.

"So late?" Though perhaps, Georgia thought, not for Venice.

"They might have come for drinks after dinner somewhere else," Millie suggested.

Cora said, "I went to bed early that time. I was excited about going to the exhibition the next day, and wanted it to come faster."

An appointment at eleven at night, and a little over twenty-four hours later, Sir Francis was dead.

"What is this business of the breakwater?" Millie asked. "Do I remember your saying that your mother is engineering a breakwater of some kind?" And Sir Francis had shushed her, lest the child be overheard in public.

"I don't know if there's going to be one for Venice," Cora confessed, riffling the corners of the right-hand pages. "But Mama is working on one for Nouveau Orléans—you know, in Nouveau France, across the sea. It's to keep the city from being flooded, or some such. But the gearworks for that are a little more complicated than airships and trains."

"Keep the city from being flooded—or act as defense?" Georgia wondered aloud. "I can see the Minister of Public Works being involved in the first, but not the second."

"If I could only see Mama, I would ask her." Cora's lip trembled just a little, but Georgia noticed.

"Darling," she said, by way of another gentle distraction, "are there any more appointments with the ministers going forward? I am certain they have heard of your father's passing and may even be at the funeral. But if not, it would be polite to let the ambassador know he must see them himself and inform them."

The girl turned pages, but other than lunches with other people and two balls hosted by English visitors to Venice, the appointments with the ministers did not appear again.

"There are two reasons I can see for this absence," Georgia confided to Millie once Cora had taken the appointment diary back up to her room. "They may schedule things on short notice, being busy men, and hadn't yet informed Sir Francis of their availability this week."

"Or they knew they would not be seeing Sir Francis again," Millie said in a low voice.

The breeze coming in the open windows bellied the sheer white curtains into the room, almost as though the villa itself were throwing up its arms in protest.

CHAPTER SEVEN

TUESDAY, MAY 7, 1895

*N*one of them, especially Cora, had thought to bring mourning clothes on their holiday to Venice. So it was that at eleven o'clock, Sir Ernest Davies-Howe escorted them into San Giuseppe d'Arimatea church in the clothes they had worn there on Sunday, with the addition of some hastily purchased black veiling with which to wreathe Cora's straw boater. Sir Ernest himself was in full dress uniform, with the rest of the diplomatic staff in black mourning coats and top hats, their medals and sashes discreetly displayed.

The Church of England funeral service was a familiar bit of home in this extraordinary place. It was also quite short, for which Georgia was thankful. "A full Venetian funeral at San Marco," Sir Ernest had whispered, "is more than two hours long, with a choir and a procession of gondolas to Isola San Michele. The nobles here think us dreadfully disrespectful in our brevity."

As Cora the deceased's nearest relative, they were obliged to sit in the front row with the ambassador and his family. That meant Georgia couldn't look about her to see who else might be in the church. Craning her neck and looking over her shoulder might have been excusable in a girl of Cora's age, but not in a woman of hers.

However, in the intervals of standing to sing and arranging one's garments after sitting, one could take in quite a lot.

"Del Campo is here," Millie breathed in her ear as they settled themselves after the second hymn. "Across the aisle and two rows back."

"And so is Mr Seacombe," Georgia whispered. "Directly behind us, near the third pillar."

"A boy is with him," Cora added.

"How do you know?" Georgia had seen no boy.

"He is holding a hat just like the one Mr Seacombe wears."

Mr Seacombe had said nothing about a boy on the two occasions they had met. Perhaps he was a member of his staff. Though the thought of Mr Seacombe having staff seemed ludicrous. He was very much the cat who walked by himself.

Georgia had to nudge Cora twice during the soliloquy. "Darling, you must not look about. You must listen to the minister."

"But what if Mama is here?"

"If she were, she would have slipped up the side of the nave and joined us."

This reply did not satisfy Cora, but at least she stopped looking back over her shoulder to examine the faces in the crowd, poor child. For it did seem rather dreadful that Lady Thorne could not be here to mourn her husband and comfort her daughter.

Had it not been for that chance meeting at the exhibition,

she and Millie would not be here, either. Would not even have heard an English diplomat was dead, only heard the bells tolling in the distance as they set off to see the next set of frescoes or visit some shop selling gloves.

When he concluded the service, the minister announced that all present were welcome at the English embassy, where luncheon would be provided for the mourners. Escorted by the ambassador himself, Georgia and her party had no chance to greet anyone in the church.

Not that she would have cornered Mr Seacombe and asked him where he had been and who his young companion was. Dear me, no. But she would have said good morning, at least. Been civil.

The embassy had, as Teddy might have said, laid on a spread in the grand reception room on the third floor. The buffet positively groaned, and people seated themselves where they liked, carrying their plates with them. Georgia took Cora outside on the balcony. It would be pleasant to obtain a little relief from those who wished to pay their respects.

"Oh, hullo," Cora said. "Auntie Georgia, we have found Mr Seacombe."

We have not been looking for Mr Seacombe.

Georgia inclined her head, and the man nodded gravely. The boy with him was already halfway through his lunch. Cora imitated him, putting her plate on the lacy stone balustrade.

"Thank you for coming to the service, Mr Seacombe," Georgia said, addressing herself to her own meal. "This is a very informal way of eating lunch, is it not?"

"Next best thing to a picnic," he said. "Kind of takes the

mind off the morning. I expect we'll have to go in and circulate soon."

The boy looked over at her plate. "What are those, ma'am?"

"Mussels," she said, spearing two and popping them in her mouth. "The Italian word for them, I am told, is *cozzi*. Delightful. And who might you be?"

"Marcus, ma'am. Marcus Seacombe."

She paused in her contemplation of her tomato and basil salad drizzled in olive oil, and glanced at the elder Mr Seacombe. "I distinctly remember you saying that you had no family, sir."

"No family waiting in the Territory," he said easily. "My son is here with me."

Millie came outside while Georgia was speechless, and handed Cora a napkin. She must have heard him, for she said the words Georgia had been trying to arrange in her mind. "You also said you had never been married."

"I haven't."

Oh. *Oh.*

"Ma died when I was three," Marcus said. "I'm eleven now. How old are you, miss?"

"I'm Cora," their charge said around an enormous olive. "I'm eleven, too. Almost. May eleventh."

"Eleven on the eleventh!" the boy said with a grin. "Mathematically, that'll never happen again." He looked up at his father. "Can I get some of those mussels, Pa?"

"May I," Cora corrected him.

"May I?"

"Yep. Bring some for me, too. I've never had 'em."

Sadly, both children had no taste for *cozzi*, so Georgia very kindly offered to take them on her own plate. Mr Seacombe, at least, braved his way through three before conceding defeat. "I guess they're an acquired taste."

"Were you hiding out here when we happened upon you?" Georgia asked.

"No, ma'am. Just catching our breath. It's a pretty view from up here, over the Piazza San Marco."

"Almost as good as the bell tower," Marcus added. "Have you been, ma'am?"

"Not yet," Millie said. "Are there very many steps?"

"No steps at all," he said eagerly. "There's a mechanical lift inside. It takes you right up to the bell platform using pulleys. You have to be careful not to go on the hour, though. The bells will make you deaf."

This would not have occurred to Georgia, but he was quite right. "One o'clock would not be so terrible, but imagine the horror of eleven."

"Exactly," Marcus said, nodding. "I made it stop at the ringers' platform, too, so I could look at the ropes they use to make them swing. I was hoping Leonardo da Vinci had invented it, but no. They told me the tower is much newer than that. Which makes no sense. Why have human bell ringers, then? A clockwork system could ring the bells as well as move the lift, couldn't it?"

"Perhaps it's a form of worship," Georgia said gently. "To make the bells ring properly is an art form. Some things are best left to people, don't you think, so they may express themselves in praise of their Creator?"

"Maybe," the boy said reluctantly. Then he brightened. "I could take you folks up there, if you haven't been yet."

"Marcus," his father said, "Miss Thorne and these ladies are in mourning. They may want to go home."

"As to that," Millie said, "we have unlimited time in which to kick our heels. The Venetian police have told us not to leave town. They are convinced that Georgia is hiding something."

"I am pretty sure her ladyship could hide nothing that would concern the police," Mr Seacombe said.

He made it sound as though she had plenty of other things to hide. "I am concealing a lover's quarrel from them, apparently," Georgia said, rather more tartly than she had intended. "They think I became incensed and may have slapped Sir Francis, causing him to go into the water."

His gaze sharpened, and she noticed for the first time that his eyes were a deep brown, like melted chocolate. "Impossible," he said flatly.

She might have felt pleased at this estimation of her character, until she realized he had probably meant the *polizia*.

"We quite agree," Millie said, finishing up her lunch. "The ambassador promises a strongly worded letter that should see the matter concluded."

"That matter, maybe," he said. "Still leaves us without a solution to the rest."

Again the plural. *Us.*

"Pa," said Marcus, "can—may I take Cora up the tower? Now?"

"Does Cora want to go?" Mr Seacombe asked. "She has just been to her father's funeral, son. She may not feel up to it."

"No point in asking her if you won't let us," the boy pointed out.

His father's moustache twitched with a smile. "You may, if Cora wishes it and Lady Langford approves."

After a moment's consideration, Cora decided she did

want to go, so Lady Langford approved. A company of adults dressed in black would only remind her of her loss, as Georgia remembered from her own mother's funeral. A few minutes of sunshine and something new would do her good, though she carried the loss with her.

"Do you have a penny for the lift?" Mr Seacombe asked his son.

"Two."

"Then we'll watch you from up here, all right?"

Georgia glanced at the chronometer pinned to her lapel. "Forty minutes until the bells ring. And only one peal. That's lucky, if they don't get down in time."

"They'll get down."

A few minutes later, the children emerged from around the corner of the embassy building. Their foreshortened figures walked across the cobbles of the square and into the door of the bell tower. Several minutes passed. Georgia was just beginning to wonder if Marcus had been distracted by the mechanics of their ascent when Mr Seacombe said, "There they are."

Two little figures waved from one of the four great arches at the top of the tower. Behind them was the bronze shape of one of the bells. Georgia and Millie waved back with energy. The figures withdrew into the shadows, where presumably Cora was going to be shown the ringers' platform.

"I am glad Cora has found a companion for today," she ventured. "The poor child is in need of something to think of besides her missing parents. While we are doing all we can for her, she has had no company but us since Wednesday. Someone of her own age will be good for her."

Mr Seacombe nodded, watching the tower. "Marcus is a

fair hand at entertaining himself, but he'll take good care of her. He's as smart as a whip, but careful, too. Gets that from his ma."

It was hardly fitting to speak of one's *affaire de coeur* to respectable ladies. Georgia decided to blame her pink cheeks on the breeze. Or a touch of sun.

"Here you are, Signorina Brunel," said a smooth voice in English behind them.

Georgia and Millie turned to find a man in an impeccably cut black linen suit and a snowy white shirt standing between the open French doors. A scarlet sash crossed his chest on the diagonal, and three medals adorned it. He stepped out on the balcony and bowed. The rings on his hands glittered in the sunlight, and when he straightened, Georgia took in the size of the square-cut ruby in his cravat pin.

They inclined their heads and Mr Seacombe touched the wide brim of his hat.

"Minister del Campo," Millie said rather breathlessly. "How kind of you to remember."

"How could I forget?"

Goodness. The man was married, was he not? Georgia was not quite prepared to play chaperone to anybody yet, never mind her husband's aunt.

"How strange it is," he went on to Millie, "that one moment we are dancing, and the next we are mourning."

"Indeed," Millie said. "But we can be grateful for friends in both such moments, can we not? Especially during the latter. Sir Ernest has been kindness itself, standing in the place of family for poor Cora Thorne."

"As are you, I understand." Eyes of so dark a brown they looked black turned his attention from Millie to Georgia, examining her from feathered hat to embellished hem. "Is she ... how do you say ... bearing up?"

"I do not know if she has fully taken it in yet," said Georgia. Neither had they. Nothing about Sir Francis washing up on their water stairs made any sense at all. "But in time, as I may say from sad experience, it will get easier."

"Ah yes. My condolences on your own bereavement, Signora." He bowed again.

"You are very kind. Will we have the pleasure of meeting your wife today, sir?"

He shook his head. "Signora del Campo does not attend events of this nature. It is more of a ... diplomatic occasion."

"Oh, of course." She supposed that representatives of the Duchy's government would turn out to pay their respects just as friends and fellow diplomats would. "I understand that your relationship with Sir Francis was very cordial."

"Indeed, Signora." His gaze slid over her face, as though curious how she had come by that information. "I find it strange, however, that the mother of the child is not here. Has some difficulty in travel prevented her attendance at her husband's funeral?"

Something in that gaze made Georgia change what she'd been about to say. "I am afraid we are completely ignorant of Lady Thorne's movements, sir. We have heard nothing. We find it as strange as you do."

He smiled, as though this were just what he had been waiting to hear. "Then perhaps my wife might serve you yet, in her small way. She would be delighted to look after the child. Our own, you see, are grown up, and she misses the chicks who were once so noisy in the nest."

Millie stepped in while Georgia was still trying to think

how to decline such a preposterous proposal without causing an international incident.

"Lady Langford will never confess it, but she feels just the same, Signore," she confided. "We find Cora's company delightful, and while it distresses us to deprive Signora del Campo of any pleasure, perhaps the child ought to stay where she is becoming comfortable. She may be upset by another change. We think it wise that she should begin to make friends with other children."

The cabinet minister bowed. "You are right, of course. Perhaps we may enjoy the pleasure of your company some evening at home. My wife is an excellent cook."

This necessitated some vague pleasantries, and a moment later he had bowed himself back inside and they were alone on their balcony.

Georgia waited a few seconds to be certain he would not reappear, then murmured, "Am I mistaken, or was that also exceedingly strange?"

"You are not mistaken," Millie murmured back.

"I think we'd be wise to collect the children and head out," Mr Seacombe suggested, his gaze raking the square below. "Hard to believe they're still up in the tower. I've had my eye on the door, but haven't seen hide nor hair of them."

The children should have been on their way back by now, or at least visible in the square, perhaps watching the jugglers or feeding the pigeons. Pulleys and gears would not have had the attraction for Cora that they had for Marcus.

"Let us take our leave as gracefully as possible, and find them," Georgia suggested. "For all we know, they may be back at the tables, helping themselves to more dessert, and we ought to prevent that at the very least."

But they were not. Sir Ernest hadn't seen them, and waved them out the door with promises of another call during the week. Neither had the children come out on the square.

"The tower it is," Millie sighed.

"Just in time to get our bells rung," Mr Seacombe said with inelegant accuracy.

Georgia could only be thankful that one o'clock rang out as they ascended in the lift, and not once they were on the topmost platform with the bells. As it was, the lift shuddered with the power of the sound. The very tower seemed to shudder. She kept her hands pressed over her ears until the last vibration faded.

They disembarked at both platforms.

No Cora. No Marcus.

"This don't make a lick of sense," Mr Seacombe growled, his voice more gravelly than usual. "Marcus wouldn't run off without telling me."

They emerged into the sunlight of the square once more. Georgia's last hope that the two miscreants would be waiting outside the door of the tower, full of apologies and a dozen good reasons for disappearing, faded into a sour, frightened feeling in her stomach.

"What is going on in this family?" she demanded of Venice in general. "First the father. Then the mother. Now Cora?"

"Does seem a bit coincidental that del Campo should come out to greet you just when we would have been watching the kids come back," Mr Seacombe said, his tone grim.

"Surely you don't suspect—" Millie began, then stopped herself. "He is a minister of the government, and a gentleman."

"Even a gentleman can be a distraction. This ain't like Marcus. Not at all. Something's happened."

"Remember the man in Cora's room the night her father died?" Georgia said suddenly. "What if he followed us here?"

"What man?" Mr Seacombe demanded.

"We have no idea," Millie said, an apology in her tone. "She said she hid, but with no more details I half thought she was dreaming."

"This is no dream, at least. We must find them," Georgia said. "I will simply not allow that child to go through anything more than she already has."

"Must we be so pessimistic?" Millie begged. "Let us go back inside and inform Sir Ernest. He will know what to do. There is always a chance they are back at the buffet by now."

Georgia turned to find Mr Seacombe's gaze upon her.

He didn't believe in chance, either.

CHAPTER EIGHT

*J*f Marcus Seacombe hadn't been pounding his fists on his captor's back, while upside down over the man's shoulder, he'd have been kicking himself for being stupid enough to get captured. In the end the man had lost his temper and walloped him, and he'd come to his senses to find himself in a coffin.

He wasn't tied up, at least. His knees were bent, his boots against a wall. With both hands, he traced out the dimensions of his prison, until his elbow nudged something soft, pressed up against his right side.

"Cora?"

She groaned. "I hit my head. Where are we? Is this the bell tower? Why is it dark?"

"This isn't the bell tower. I thought it was a coffin, but it's too short. It's a chest. Smell."

She sniffed at the faint odor. "Cinnamon. And seaweed. What happened?"

"I don't know. Somebody grabbed us at the bottom of the lift."

"But why?"

"Don't know that, either."

"It doesn't matter. We have to escape. Mama may have come and I must go home with Auntie Georgia." Her voice was becoming stronger. "Is it a hasp lock, or a mechanical one?"

Because of course their small prison was locked. Nobody put people in a spice chest without locking it. "What difference does it make?"

"Just tell me. The hinges are on this side. I can feel them. So the lock must be on yours."

He investigated, his fingers finding a metal mechanism about where a hasp would be. "Mechanical."

"Good. Trade me places."

He went under, like a gentleman, and she rolled overtop of him. His stomach rolled, too, as the bottom of the chest tilted and wobbled, as unstable as could be. "Be careful! We're in the water."

She froze, and gingerly they rearranged themselves in a gently rocking balance. "Please tell me we're in a boat, and not floating like Moses in his basket."

It seemed no one was coming to see why the boat was rocking. "Must be," he ventured. "A chest in a boat. What are you going to do?"

"Pick the lock from behind."

He drew a sharp breath. "Just like An Educated Gentleman in *Tales of a Medicine Man*!" Why hadn't he thought of that?

"Exactly. We have the *Illustrated News* sent to the Kastanienhof every month from London. Mama loves the *Tales*. And the illustrations are topping." Something was making clicking noises. "This was in the one where he escapes with the princess from the sinking prison ship. Remember? They floated out in a coffin—but it accidentally locked on them because it wasn't a coffin after all. It was a gun chest."

"I remember. Locked in a gun chest in the ocean. And we had to wait until the *next issue* to find out what happened. What's that noise?"

"One of my hairpins."

Of course it was. Girls had a distinct advantage in having somewhere to conceal useful equipment.

While she worked, he listened hard. Their captors had exchanged few words, but they must have gone, since no one seemed to be coming to investigate a rocking, talking spice chest.

There ought to be some identifiable noise. All right, the lapping of water. But not the lapping he was familiar with—against a canoe or rowboat. Not a steamship, either. It was a hollow sound he'd been hearing ever since he and Pa had arrived.

The sound of water against the heavy hull of a gondola. They were still in Venice, at least.

"We're in a gondola," he whispered, so as not to disturb her concentration very much. "Moored, I think. And not in a small backwater canal. Somewhere with waves. So, other boats and wind. People to help us, maybe."

"Or hurt us. Will we be spotted when we get out?" she whispered back.

When was a cheerful word. "We'll have to go over the side, and be quick about it."

"We can't go over the side!" she hissed. "What about the krakens?"

"The what now?"

"The big canals are full of krakens! I'm not going in there to be eaten!"

"That's just a story to keep little kids away from the water." The boys in the street had threatened to throw him to the krakens, but he'd thought they were just being idiots. "Dad's friend in the monastery says there are stories of the creatures saving people from drowning."

"That can't be true," she insisted, still working on the lock. "It's why people don't escape from cleaning the gearworks when they're condemned to prison. *I've* heard the krakens get them if they try."

Maybe the rattlers and scorpions at home weren't so bad. They might bite or sting, but at least they wouldn't eat you.

There was a *click*. Cora exhaled with satisfaction and lay back next to him, pushing her hairpin back into her hair. He heard the tiny scrape on her scalp. "Now we have to make a plan."

"We'll lift the lid. Slowly. Just a crack. So we can see where we are."

The lid was heavy, but using hands and feet, they tilted it up just enough to see ...

... nothing. It was dark. And still the water lapped at the hull.

"Push," he whispered. "I'll hold the lid for you while you climb out. Then you hold it for me."

In less than a minute they were out of the spice chest. He lowered the lid soundlessly and pressed the mechanism so that it locked once more. "I know what this is. A gondola with one of those cabins. You know, that the nobility use."

Velvet drapes covered the windows, and the upholstery

was as soft as a feather bed. The chest lay on the parquet floor between two seats covered in red velvet pillows.

"Look." She pointed to the heraldic arms embroidered in gold thread on one of the pillows. "The lion of Venice, the Medici crown, and the field of valor. Del Campo."

"How do you know?"

"Diplomat's daughter. We went to his house once and the arms are everywhere. *Campo* means field. His family helped the Doge win some big battle hundreds of years ago."

"I wonder what del Campo wants with us?"

But there was no answer to that. He cracked the curtains and recognized the island across the water. The ever-changing map of Venice turned itself right way up in his head. "We're near the Arsenale. Come on. We'll have to swim."

"But the krak—"

"Do you want to be murdered like your dad?" She gasped, but there was no time to apologize for his tendency to brutal honesty. "We'll have to risk it."

He went over the side with barely a splash, and trod water until she slid in beside him, her skirts floating up around her chest.

"Stay low."

The grand gondola was moored at a private pier in front of a huge pink wedding cake of a villa, surrounded by several vessels just like it. Either the rich people were having a sunset party with lots of guests, or the vessels were being used as camouflage. In either case, common folk weren't likely to be coming by looking for a ride.

The canal was a pretty big one. And deep—he couldn't touch bottom. Would krakens come in this close?

He could only hope they would not. They must find a busy

fondamente and people and *vaporetti* to stir up the water, but quick.

Ducking to swim underwater below the hulls, slipping soundlessly away from the gilded posts where the gondolas were tied up, they worked their way around the point toward the Arsenale, where the Duchy stored its bombs and guns in case of invasion. With every second, he expected a tentacle to wrap itself around his ankle and pull him down. When they were finally able to find a narrow, shallow canal that allowed them to find their footing and then climb an iron ladder on to the *fondamente*, it was all he could do not to whimper with gratitude. Away from the Arsenale he made a camouflaging zigzag of running down lanes and between buildings until they reached the fish market by the Ponte Rialto.

Dripping and bedraggled as she was, Cora still turned up her nose. "It smells!"

The fishmongers had gone home. The flagstones were still wet from the melted ice in the deserted stalls, with fish heads and dead eels littering the ground. Already the gulls and cats were taking care of the problem. By nightfall it would all be gone.

He wrung out the tails of his shirt while she did the same with her dress. "Of course it smells, after all day in the sun. They bring in the fish at four in the morning. Come on."

At the big blue door behind which home lay, he pressed the studs in the lock. When it opened, he and Cora slipped into the courtyard. Their shoes made puddles on the stone stairs up to the flat he and Pa shared. They smelled, too, of the black mud on the bottom of the canals.

But they'd given their captors the slip!

He laughed out loud as he pressed the combination to the

mechanical lock on their own door, then opened the door of the flat and ushered Cora inside.

"We're alive!" he exulted, and grabbed her hand. "Well done for getting us out of that chest."

"Well done for getting us here," she said, and gave him a smacking kiss on the cheek.

His face flashed hot with embarrassment and he dropped her hand. "We'd better get cleaned up. I'll ask the signora downstairs if we can use her copper bath. And she'll wash our clothes. Pa's client pays her to take care of us."

She stopped gazing around her at the white plaster walls and cheerful crockery that the signora supplied her tenants. "This isn't your home?"

"For now, while Pa guards his client. He lives on the other side of the courtyard."

"Guards? Is he a prisoner?"

Marcus grinned while he hunted up blankets and indicated she should remove her wet things. "No, he's a multimillionaire. We came in his private airship—practically as big as *Persephone*, it is. He's here making some big deal with the Duchy and a bunch of other people. Pa is his bodyguard. It's all very hush-hush. No one is supposed to know, so you can't tell."

She stared at him as she took the blanket and drew it around her shoulders. "A Texican multimillionaire … it can't be the Stanford Fremonts. Is your father guarding Mr van Meere? The railroad baron?"

How in tarnation did she know that? So much for hush-hush. He collected their wet clothes and put them in a basket. "How did you know it was him?"

"He called on Mama a while ago, in his big ship. He had to

moor it at the Theresienwiese fairgrounds—it wouldn't fit at the airfield. Are you in danger? For being with him? Since he needs a bodyguard?"

"I've never been in any danger, Cora. Not until I met you."

She opened her mouth, and closed it again. "I'm sorry. I didn't mean for us to be kidnapped. I've never been in any danger, either, until I came here."

"You can tell me what you mean after we bathe. Come on."

The signora tut-tutted over them as, one after the other, they washed in her copper bath behind a curtain, but said she would have their clothes laundered and dried as fast as the steam boiler could work.

Then they ran back upstairs wrapped in their blankets. He put their shoes out on the stoop to dry, and they settled at the pine table with some orange juice from the icebox, and the contents of the cookie tin. Nothing had ever tasted so good.

"Now, what's this danger you were talking of?"

Her mouth full of iced shortbread, she said, "Last week a man broke into my room, and the next morning Papa was dead. Now we've been kidnapped." She washed the cookie down with orange juice. "This is very good. I thought I would like Venice, but I really don't." Her lower lip trembled. "I want Mama. And Papa back again. And for things to be the way they were, at Kastanienhof."

He could handle a lot of things, but a crying girl was not one of them. Even if he sympathized.

"Broke into your room?" he said hastily, and gave her one of the table napkins. "What did you do?"

She blew her nose, and seemed to collect herself. "I slid out of the bed, between it and the wall, and crawled underneath. He tossed the blankets about, but when he couldn't find me, he went out the bedroom door. I was so frightened I couldn't move, and woke up in the morning still on the floor. Later Auntie Georgia and Auntie Millie came, and told me what happened to Papa." Her eyes widened. "You don't think that man killed Papa because he was angry he couldn't find me, do you?"

He shook his head, and did the only thing he could think of—offered her another piece of shortbread, this one iced to look like a house. "The two things must be connected. But I don't see how your dad's drowning at Lady Langford's house could be your fault. It's just awful luck, is all."

"Maybe." But she didn't seem convinced. "This is a terrible adventure. Papa promised me it would be fun. And now look. I can't even go home to Kastanienhof ... unless I run away."

"Look on the bright side," he said, before that thought could take root. "We got away from those men. Think how mad they'll be when they unlock that chest and find it empty."

At last, a smile brightened her face. "Mad—oh, you mean angry. We still don't know who they are. Maybe they work for Signore del Campo. He scares me. Papa let me stay up to meet him one time when he came to dinner, and then today, at the church, he gave me a lemon drop from his pocket. But it was sour. Not like a real sweet at all."

Marcus bit back the urge to point out that at this rate, she was lucky it hadn't been poisoned.

"We don't know exactly who kidnapped us," he said instead. "All we know is that they hid the spice chest on one of his gondolas. But if it wasn't on purpose, they were taking an awful risk hiding us there. What if someone wanted to go somewhere? They might have tossed us overboard."

She nodded. "Auntie Georgia will be so worried."

He glanced at the sky, which was red and violet with the last of the sunset over the rooftops. In the deep blue above, the evening star glimmered. "Knowing Pa, he's already tearing Venice apart looking for us."

"He won't be angry, will he?" She looked anxious.

"Not at us," he assured her. "He'll be glad we're safe and sound. But I can't say the same for whoever snatched us. I wouldn't want to be them for all the gold in El Dorado."

GEORGIA WAS FAR TOO familiar with the outward manifestations of rage. The heavy footfall. The too emphatic gesture. The flinging out of the arm, which more often than not connected painfully. Mr Seacombe in a rage, however, was unlike anything in her previous experience. His movements were fluid, contained, as though he were a kind of panther stalking the lanes and alleyways of Venice.

A silent, vengeful figure making his way across Venice by the fastest route.

Millie had protested at having to stay behind at the Villa dei Pappagalli, but as Mr Seacombe tersely pointed out, if the children returned there, they would need to be looked after, and word sent immediately by Lorenzo to Mr Seacombe's lodgings. That was their destination now.

"What if they are not there?" Georgia was practically running, trying to keep up with his ground-eating stride and not trip over a slate or a cobblestone in the fading light.

He looked over his shoulder, and, seeing that she was having difficulty, slowed his furious pace. "We'll jump off that bridge when we get to it," he said, his voice more gravelly than ever. "Your villa and ours are the first two places to eliminate from the list."

"And what possibilities remain once we do that?"

"We'll have to think on it," he said. "I have an idea or two. I reckon you do as well."

But having an idea and having proof were vastly different.

"You do not think it coincidental that in the few minutes our eyes were off them and on del Campo, they disappeared." She was being silly. Of course the two events had nothing to do with one another.

"I don't believe in coincidence, my lady."

Oh, dear. Could any reply be more terrifying?

The fact was, del Campo's name and elegant person were coming up far too often. If the children were not at the Seacombe lodgings, she did not feel herself adequate to bearding the cabinet minister in his opulent den, and demanding to know if his wife had satisfied her wish for a chick in the nest against Cora's will. But if it meant the lives and safety of the children, then she would do what had to be done, and the devil take the hindmost.

"Nearly there," he said, slowing even more and offering his arm. "Time to look as though we're not—"

"Panicked?"

"I was going to say in a hurry."

"*You* may not be in a hurry. *I* am panicked."

"Save it until we find out if they're here. Drop the veil on your hat, if you please. It might be nearly dark, but I'd rather the neighbors didn't recognize my guest."

The words, *Do you often have female guests in the evening?* crowded her tongue, but with an admirable exercise of control, she bit them back. It was none of her business. So she merely unfurled the navy net chin veil from around the crown of her hat, and lowered it into place, as she had during the funeral service. She could see through it perfectly well, but to an onlooker, her features would be indistinct, especially at a distance and in poor light.

It was a widow's veil, and did its job well.

He pressed several of the studs on an ornate mechanical lock and opened the heavy, carved street door, which admitted them to a private courtyard. Hanging lanterns were strung above from veranda to veranda. Lemon trees in large terracotta pots dotted the tiles, and flowers in baskets hung from the exposed beams of the loggia down one side. He led the way to an external stair and motioned for her to precede him. Small lamps sat on every third step, burning brightly.

Two steps up, she bent to peer at the slate. "They are here."

He examined the muddy footprint, dry now and pale on the spotless slate. A long breath escaped him. "That simplifies things."

They followed the prints up the dozen stairs to a simple wooden door. He reached past her to rap a syncopated, brief tattoo upon it. A coded knock. Now, why should a father and son need a coded knock in so very secure a home?

A flurry of footsteps, and the door was wrenched open. "Dad!"

Mr Seacombe scooped the boy into a fierce hug as he crossed the threshold. Georgia had barely got herself inside and off the high, bannister-less stoop before Cora flung herself into her arms.

"Oh, Auntie Georgia, I'm so glad to see you! It was so awful. They put us in a spice chest but I picked the lock from the inside and then we had to swim and there are krakens, you know, and Marcus was so clever, he knew exactly where he was and then the signora washed our clothes!"

Georgia dried her own wet cheeks with a quick swipe of her lawn sleeve. "How very kind of her," she said in a voice that was almost normal. "Marcus, thank you and the signora both for looking after Cora."

"She looked after me," the boy said, his arms tight around his father's waist. "She can pick a lock like anything, ma'am. And she was only a little afraid of the krakens."

"So were you!" Cora said.

"I sure was," he confessed baldly. "I thought they were a fairytale."

"They aren't. But neither are they predators. Come and sit down. Tell us everything," Mr Seacombe instructed.

Fifteen minutes later Georgia's blood had run cold, then hot, then cold again. When the two children had run out of breath, she looked up to find Mr Seacombe's gaze on her.

"It might've been a coincidence, our being distracted," he said, as though continuing their previous conversation. "But with timing like that, I doubt it. The gearworks for the bell tower's lift are underground. There's an access tunnel from there to the church. No wonder we didn't see them come out." He shook his head at himself. "Ought to have been the first place I looked."

"How do you know?" Cora asked him. "About the tunnel?"

"It's my job to know."

"Ah." She nodded wisely. "In case somebody tries to snatch Mr van Meere. They'd have a time getting *him* over their shoulder, wouldn't they?"

Dustin Seacombe had frozen at the mention of his

employer's name. Then, as though he were an automaton, his head swivelled to level an accusing glare at his son.

"I'm sorry, Pa. She already knew. He's visited them in Munich."

Now that glare turned on Cora, who did not flinch. "You know Cornelius van Meere?"

"He came to visit Mama and was ever so long in the laboratory with her. Till after midnight. He went away before I even woke up."

"When was this?"

Her brow crinkled in thought. "I'm not sure. Just after examinations—oh! It was just before Christmas. I remember because we went to the Christkindlmarkt the next night and I was so sleepy we came home early. But at least I had a present for Papa." Her eyes took on a faraway expression, as though remembering happier times.

"This past Christmas?"

She came back to herself and nodded. "Is that bad?"

He seemed to shake himself. "No, child. It's just new information. Has nothing to do with what you two have been through. Marcus, can you run down and ask the signora to send word to Miss Brunel that the two of you are here? And let her know we'll be four for supper."

"Yessir. Come on, Cora. Let's see what she's making."

The children ran out, and over the clatter of dried shoes going down the steps, Georgia said, "The resilience of youth. I should be prostrate for a week if I had been kidnapped and had to escape in such a fashion."

"Ah, but you aren't a spy." The corner of his mouth twitched up in a smile.

"Certainly not. Of all the children in Venice to kidnap, our perpetrator certainly chose the wrong ones."

"I'm proud of them. Marcus has a natural bent for tinkering that has saved us a time or two. Cora's mother seems to have raised a daughter with resources, and the courage to use them."

She eyed him. "You do not credit her father?"

He shrugged. "Don't know her father at all, except as your dance partner. And a good friend of Minister del Campo."

Goodness. She had quite forgotten. "That reminds me— the ambassador brought Sir Francis's appointment diary to Cora, along with his effects. In it we found a number of extracurricular meetings with del Campo. Dinners and late-evening drinks. That sort of thing."

"Did you, now?" His gaze intensified. "This is Venice. Not so unusual. But still. Anything else?"

"Sir Francis used initials, so Cora helped us with the ones she knew. Alessandro di Narbone joined them once or twice, including the very night before the exhibition opened. He is the Conte di Narbone's cousin, apparently."

"He is." He ruminated for a moment. "So the Minister of Public Works met privately several times with an English diplomat whose specialty is trade and technology, along with the man famous for not getting a railroad into Venice."

"Hardly his fault," Georgia pointed out.

"True. Old Leonardo didn't anticipate trains when he built the gearworks."

"Cora was listening under the window, and told us that their conversation was mainly about airships and transfer taxes. Dishes, apparently, were smashed. I had no idea taxes could provoke such passion in the human heart."

"Smashed by whom, I wonder?" Mr Seacombe murmured.

"Does it matter?"

"Well, if del Campo was smashing dishes, I'd reckon the Duchy was about to enter a war. Sir Francis? Probably just dropped one. Di Narbone? Frustration at being denied some other harebrained scheme."

"Like the breakwater." She nodded.

Once more that deep brown gaze fixed on her face. It was dashed uncomfortable being the sole object of such intense scrutiny. "What do you know about that?"

"Only that Cora said it was also part of the conversation."

"Before or after smashing the dishes?"

"I don't remember. We'll ask her when they come back upstairs. Does it matter?"

He relaxed against the back of the settee, and she found her own spine settling once again into the cushions of the wing chair she occupied. "It might. My client and Cora's mother share an interest in that project."

"Let us hope that is all they share." At his raised eyebrow, she said, "She is missing, if you recall."

"Not merely in transit?"

"The embassy checked. Between last Wednesday, when we discovered Sir Francis, and Sunday at church, when I asked the ambassador, no tickets on any mode of transportation had been purchased in her name."

"She might have used an alias. I have a hard time believing Cora's mother is unaware of her husband's death, and isn't coming for her."

"I cannot believe that, either. In fact—"

A return clatter of leather soles, and the children ran back in. Marcus handed Georgia a note. "From Villa dei Pappagalli, ma'am."

"The signora's son couldn't have taken my message there and back so fast," Mr Seacombe objected.

"Lorenzo brought it," Cora said. "He's our gondolier. He's waiting below for a reply."

Millie had folded the note in her most complicated design. One meant to slow any reader but the one intended so much that they either tore it in frustration or were caught red-handed, both of which would prove they were being a sneak. But Georgia knew the octagonal fold well. Heaven knew they had used it often enough at Langford Park.

"I must get Auntie Millie to show me how to do that," Cora whispered to Marcus.

Georgia—

I am dreadfully worried. Please send word by Lorenzo to let me know you are all right. No sign of the children yet.

Something strange has occurred. The gondola in which Sir Francis met his end is gone. I do not know when. When I went out to give Lorenzo this note, he asked me if I had ordered it removed. Of course we had not.

Do you think we ought to put a lock on the macaw's door? For the egg in his nest is now the only evidence that anything untoward occurred.

Millie

CHAPTER NINE

*L*orenzo had been dispatched to fetch Miss Brunel, and the signora informed that there would be five, not four, for supper. In return, that lady sent up the children's freshly laundered garments. Georgia did not ask how the reclusive Mr van Meere took his meals, but she did observe a boy with a tray going up the staircase on the opposite side of the courtyard. That must be why Mr Seacombe was able to devote his time to his present company. His services as bodyguard were evidently not needed this evening.

When she arrived, Millie hugged both children fiercely, and was regaled with the tale of their escape until the signora and her nearly grown children came in bearing trays. Dinner was creamy noodles that Georgia learned were called *linguine*, studded with fat shrimp and cut-up asparagus and tiny brown mushrooms, with a salad and a delicious broiled fish. It was all washed down with a delightful white wine that apparently came from the signora's brother's vineyard in Tuscany.

She really must convince Teddy that they required an

Italian cook at the town house. Even if she gained twenty pounds in the first month.

Over dinner, Millie gave an additional detail or two about the missing gondola. "Lorenzo said that after we left for the funeral, when he took his mother to the market, the gondola was still tied up at the water stairs. When he returned, it was gone, but he thought nothing of it. The only thing he thought odd was that we had not asked him to take it back to the manufactory so that it could be returned."

"We don't know who it belonged to," Georgia objected. "How could it be returned?"

"Apparently Signore Barcaiolo, the master, has his ways. There is some sort of lost and found arrangement," Millie said. "Lorenzo has asked them to inform him if it turns up there."

"Good thinking," Mr Seacombe said.

Georgia had formed a conviction that was fast becoming a certainty. "We have two possibilities. The first is that Minister del Campo removed it, but of course we have no proof of that. I favor the second possibility—that the Long and the Short of it had the gondola removed."

"The who?" This time both Mr Seacombe's eyebrows rose.

"The two policemen who informed us we are practically prisoners here while dear Georgia is under suspicion," Millie said.

"They cannot think Auntie Georgia killed Papa," Cora said around a particularly large shrimp. "They barely knew each other. And besides, she's lovely."

Georgia's heart melted at the girl's confidence in her after so short but eventful an acquaintance. "Even if they did think so, the Ambassador is going to tell them to lift their order," she said. "That's why I think the *polizia* carried off the gondola. They've been instructed to cease and desist, and take their evidence with them."

"Then why not tell Signore Airone?" Millie said. "Why wait until the house was nearly empty and do it on the sly?"

"I have a question in addition to that one," Mr Seacombe said. "How did they remove it with no oar? And did anyone wonder where said oar was?"

"The last the Long and the Short of it saw, it was lying on the *fondamente*," Georgia told him. "Perhaps they think it was knocked into the water and floated away on the tide."

"Sloppy," he said. "But all the same, I'm glad they didn't mount a search for it."

"The fewer who know of it, the better," Georgia said firmly. "So without an oar, how did they remove that vessel?"

"Someone could have brought an extra," Marcus said. "Or a rope to tow it with."

"Which brings us back to an older question," Millie said. "We still do not know how Sir Francis or the gondola came to be at our water stairs. That reminds me—Cora, did your papa know how to steer such a vessel?"

The girl's smile flashed again. "Papa did not even know how to swim. The canals were the one thing he hated about Venice. Every time he left the house, he was convinced he would be tipped out of the gondola and pulled under by a kraken—or lose his balance and drown."

The silence drew into a fine thread of tension. Was there such a thing as presentiment? Georgia believed so.

"So if the gondola and oar and Sir Francis were all there, and Sir Francis did not steer himself, then what happened to the gondolier?" Marcus said, clearly objecting to the illogic of it.

"If we knew that, we'd have our murderer, I suspect," his father said. "It's the question that's been a burr under my saddle for a week."

"We'll probably never know," Georgia mused. "But if the Long and the Short of it appear tomorrow to inform me I am no longer suspected of killing Cora's papa in a lovers' quarrel, I think we can infer that they made off with the gondola themselves, and are not going to bother finding the oar, to say nothing of a murderous gondolier."

"Another burr. Why bury the case with no investigation?" Mr Seacombe asked.

"It's not very fair to Cora's pa," Marcus said. "A murderer strolling around Venice free as a bird and no one doing a blessed thing about it."

"I quite agree," Millie said. "For Cora's sake, however, we have done what we could." She smiled tenderly at the girl and squeezed her shoulders.

"Here is another burr for our metaphorical saddle," Georgia said. "Why should dear Cora suffer kidnap attempts both the night of and a week *after* her father's death? One hears of such terrible things—the innocent child being taken to extort a ransom from the parent. But if the parent were already out of the game, what is the point?"

Mr Seacombe was gazing at her with admiration. She pretended not to notice.

"Maybe," he said slowly, "we're looking at the wrong parent."

"You think those men in the bell tower wanted to kidnap Marcus, not me?" Cora's brows wrinkled in confusion.

"The number of people who know about my purpose here are all within steps of that door," Mr Seacombe said, hooking a thumb at the entrance to their cheery apartment. "I think it's safe to say you were the target, Cora, and they took Marcus thinking he was simply a playmate, so he wouldn't raise the alarm."

"Which I would have," the boy assured Cora. "If they hadn't knocked me on the noggin."

Georgia slid a glance at Mr Seacombe's face and saw the unknown kidnapper's fate written in those fathomless eyes, should the former ever lay hands on him.

"And do not forget that peculiar offer by Minister del Campo," Millie put in. To Cora, she said, "He invited you rather pointedly to stay at his home in his wife's care until your mother arrived. She is lonely since their children have left home, he said."

The girl made a face as though she had smelled decomposing fish. "I don't want to stay with Signore del Campo, even if he did give me a lemon drop. I named all the parakeets in my room when I couldn't sleep. I want to stay with you and Auntie Georgia."

"I am very glad to hear it," Georgia told her with a smile. "So that's three people since Wednesday who have wanted you in their hands rather than ours. Now, why should that be? Is there some state secret you know, darling? Something you overheard that could jeopardize them in some way?"

"Like a treasure map?" Marcus said hopefully. "Something in the villa where you lived?"

"No," Cora said sadly. "The only thing interesting about the Villa dei Delfini was the chicken coop on the roof. The cook keeps them for the eggs."

"And you've told us what you remember of your father's conversations over dinner with Signore del Campo," Georgia said. "Which reminds me—on the night before the exhibition, when the minister and Signore di Narbone were at dinner and you were under the window, you said they spoke of the breakwater."

Cora nodded, twirling up the last of her linguine on her fork.

"Did they start breaking dishes *after* that came up, or before, when they were talking about transfer taxes?"

"After." The girl tilted her head. "Nobody breaks dishes over taxes."

Georgia considered the airship captains facing prison for refusing to pay them. "Perhaps not at dinner. Mr Seacombe, does that answer your question?"

"Gives me something to think on besides burrs and how full I am," he said, tilting his chair back on its hind legs in a most unsafe manner. "A breakwater out there in the lagoon, hey? Is that enough to make people break dishes?"

"When Mama comes, we will ask her," Cora said. "She knows more about breakwaters than anyone. And dishes, too, probably."

"Mr van Meere is handy," Marcus suggested. "He seems to know about breakwaters."

"Don't you go bothering Mr van Meere," his father said with abrupt sternness. "I'll take that up with him myself. I'm supposed to attend him to a meeting tomorrow."

"With whom?" Millie asked. "Are we permitted to know?"

"Nope." Mr Seacombe let his chair come back to the horizontal with a thump. "Lady Langford, I wonder if you might consider allowing Cora to stay here for a day or two."

Cora left off wriggling, as though she was actually about to imitate her host's treatment of his chair. "Leave the Villa dei Pappagalli?" She took Millie's hand. "I don't want to."

"Think about it," Marcus said. "What if a man comes in the night again?"

"Marcus, don't frighten her," Mr Seacombe growled.

"I am not frightened," Cora said. "But Auntie Georgia and Auntie Millie said they would look after me."

"Cora, consider," Georgia said slowly. "No one knows where Marcus lives."

"Lorenzo does," the child objected.

"We trust Lorenzo. But several people we do *not* trust know where you live at the moment, first among them being Minister del Campo. I wonder if perhaps you would be safer here, just for a short while."

Mr Seacombe said, "If we get a bit of luck and the bridges go up, it might slow down a search even more."

"I'll do my best not to let us be kidnapped again," Marcus said earnestly.

Cora looked from one to the other. Then, to Marcus, she said, "Do you promise?"

"I do. And I can show you the chickens on our roof. Our signora keeps them, too, and they're ever so nice."

"I like chickens. Can anybody see us up there?"

"No, there's a grape arbor growing out of pots that covers it. But we can still see out. I'll show you tomorrow."

The chickens seemed to settle it. Georgia squashed the niggle of worry that insisted on living beneath her breastbone. Mr Seacombe was a man of the law. Mr van Meere seemed to have resources they did not, and was known to

Cora's family besides. It really did seem the safest course of action for the girl.

Georgia exchanged a glance with Millie, and saw acceptance in her eyes. "Very well," she said. "Shall we say two days? In that time hopefully we will untangle this knot and find out what on earth is going on."

"If Lady Thorne turns up in the meantime, then of course we will deliver Cora to her instantly," Millie added.

"Agreed," Mr Seacombe said. "I'll have a word with my friend at the monastery after I see Mr van Meere to his meeting. He might have heard something."

Mr Seacombe came back with them to collect Cora's traveling closet, which fortunately contained another hat, since she had lost hers while being carried over a miscreant's shoulder. Before he and Georgia went back downstairs to Millie and Lorenzo, who were waiting at the water stairs, they checked the macaw's closet to make certain the oar was still there.

It was. On impulse, Georgia added Sir Francis's appointment diary to the shelf above it, pushing it all the way to the back. "I will ask Cora's forgiveness for taking her property when next I see her."

"Doesn't hurt to be cautious," he said. "As for seeing her, when might that be?"

Georgia had already given this some thought. She closed the closet door and leaned on it. "We ought to keep congress between our two houses to a minimum. You may not be easy to follow, but Millie and I have no experience with such things. In travel back and forth, we may inadvertently guide the men from the bell tower to her."

There was no light except for the lamp she'd carried

upstairs and set on the bureau, and that of similar lamps in the rooms of the villa across the canal. All the same, she detected a smile in his voice. "Congress, my lady?"

She immediately regretted her choice of words. And he had no business saying *my lady* like that. Or of somehow managing it so that they were alone for the first time in their acquaintance.

Resolutely, she kept the conversation on the rails of propriety.

"Congress, visits, traffic—call it what you like, we should not draw attention in that way. Today has been the longest I have ever experienced. If it suits you, perhaps Millie and I will wait a little, and come Friday?"

He inclined his head. "Dinner? I will let the signora know."

"Thank you." She took a step away. "We must go down. I don't like to keep Millie waiting in the night air."

"My lady." He touched her wrist, and she could feel it like a catspaw of wind upon the water, through her lace cuff and all the way to her shoulder. "Be careful. Something dangerous is on that little girl's trail. I don't want to see you or Miss Brunel hurt."

"Thank you," she murmured. "You be careful, too."

Then she turned and led the way down to safety.

CHAPTER TEN

WEDNESDAY, MAY 8, 1895

*A*s had become their habit, Georgia and Millie took their breakfast upon the balcony off the sitting room, overlooking their new prospect since the last turn of the neighborhoods.

"What a pity," Millie said, scanning the rooftops. "We are now facing north, and the sun does not reach here as it did before."

"On the other hand, it saves us from having to wear hats to breakfast," Georgia pointed out.

The appalling events of yesterday and the silence of the villa today seemed to have left the larger world unaffected. Below, a gondolier steered his vessel in solitude. On the larger canals, vessels passed one another to each side, as though marine rules existed governing right of way. But this canal was fairly narrow. Without the glare of light on the water, one could see unexpected details. Georgia sipped her *cappuccino* and watched the lazy plumes of mud stirred up by the oar as the gondola made its way past the villa and on toward the rectangle of bright light at the end, several villas down, where busy boatmen plied the larger canal.

She blinked. Mud.

"Millie, look there, in the water behind that gondola."

Obligingly, Millie turned in her wrought-iron chair, but now the light was wrong. The reflections rippled on the surface, no longer making it possible to see what Georgia had seen.

"Never mind, dearest. How deep do you suppose these little canals are?"

Millie shook her head. "I have no idea. We can see seven of our water stairs, but I do not know if they rest upon the bottom or not. And with the neighborhoods changing, a canal could be one depth and width one day and another the next."

"The children's shoes were muddy, you recall, when they reached Mr Seacombe's lodgings."

"A natural consequence, surely, when one swims with them on, and then runs on land?"

"Yes, but dust and street dirt would shake off as the shoes dried. Cora's shoes were *coated*. We shall have to see she gets new ones—those were her best black patents, for church."

"Coated with mud." Millie gazed over her cup at the canal below, following its calm glimmer. "Are you saying the children walked down a canal during their escape?"

"We will ask, but it seems possible. Millie, we have been asking ourselves what on earth could have happened to Sir Francis's gondolier that night. What if, after he made certain the poor man was dead, he simply abandoned ship and—"

"—walked away," Millie breathed. "Or, if the canal were not as shallow as this, he could even have swum."

"A loose, unadorned gondola would have been returned to

the manufactory's lost and found to await its owner's inquiries, and would never be connected to a murder. Certainly, if not for Lorenzo's resourcefulness, we ourselves would never have known its original purchaser."

"As Mr Seacombe would say, sloppy," Millie said dryly. "Who leaves the murder weapon lying in plain sight?"

"Perhaps they were counting on the tide, or the bridges going up, and miscalculated," Georgia said. "Perhaps Sir Francis *was* coming to see me—not for *that*," she said hastily at the scandalized look on Millie's face. "I was quite clear that I was not the sort to carry on with a married man. The gondolier realized he was running out of time, did the terrible deed, and walked away, leaving all behind in the water. The krakens might have taken care of a body, and the tide the rest."

But Millie was already frowning. "It seems rather slapdash, don't you think? A crime of opportunity rather than one carefully planned. And if a canal is shallow, how would a kraken get in? How big are they?"

"Big enough to eat someone?" Georgia had never seen one, and by God's grace, never would. "Hence their effectiveness at preventing prisoners from escaping the gearworks. What a dreadful, barbarous custom."

Millie put her fork down, as though she had lost her appetite for the remainder of her spinach and cheese omelette. "So leaving out the krakens, it seems to me that our gondolier—"

"Or whoever sent him."

"Quite right. They succeed no matter what. If the tide takes away the evidence, well and good. If it doesn't, Sir Francis is found floating at your doorstep, and you are a convenient person to blame it on."

"Which was exactly what happened." Georgia laid down her own fork. "They did not factor our acquaintance with the ambassador into that calculation, however. I wonder if the dogs will be called off the hunt?"

"Let us hope so," Millie said. "Truly, dear, I am really beginning to think we ought to book a stateroom for three on an airship going to Bavaria. And sooner rather than later."

"Three attempts at removing Cora from our loving arms is a bit much to put up with, I agree."

"Mind you, if Lady Thorne persists in being missing, I am not certain what good it will do Cora. She will be at home in Munich, true, but with only the staff. Not her family. I would not feel right simply leaving her there."

"Nor would I," Georgia admitted. "I fully realize Lady Thorne may have met the same fate as her husband. But leaving that out for the time being, how does one find a woman who does not wish to be found? Assuming that similar attempts have been made to kidnap her."

"I do not know," Millie said. "It is not like setting out into the garden to find a missing hen."

Georgia could well imagine that trying to answer such a question could lead to a dark room and a cold cloth upon one's forehead.

"One thing at a time," she told her companion. "For now, I am going out on the *fondamente* to paint."

"Paint?" Millie laid down her napkin and rose. "With people's lives in danger all around us, you are going to *paint*?"

"Indeed I am. And you should, too. We cannot walk about as tourists, looking over our shoulders every moment. If anyone should come along to make inquiries, they will find us productively occupied and looking every bit as innocent as we claim to be."

Millie nodded, looking doubtful.

"What's more, if our thinking is right, I predict that the Long and the Short of it will arrive soon. I am determined they shall not find us half mad with the strain, screaming and shaking our fists at imaginary krakens."

Not long afterward, the Long and the Short of it *did* turn up, before Millie had done much more than sketch in the outlines of a particularly attractive wrought-iron water gate now located on the opposite side of the canal.

At least she was not yet covered in daubs of paint. For her, watercolor was a messy business, but at least it was ladylike and easily washed off. Millie had often been glad that Georgia had not convinced her to take up oil paints. The chaos that would have resulted from *that* choice made her orderly mind shudder away in horror. As it was, she and Georgia had only to remove their pinafore aprons and seat themselves on the sofa in the sitting room before Signore Airone showed the two policemen in.

"Signora, Signorina," Short, the senior man, greeted them. "I hope we find you well this morning."

"Very well, thank you," Millie responded in Italian. "Do sit down. To what do we owe the honor of this visit?"

"Good news, I trust," Long said, declining to sit. "We will not stay long. Our investigation has concluded, and we are here to inform you that you are free to leave Venice whenever you choose. Though of course we hope you will stay a little longer, to enjoy its many beauties."

Millie translated swiftly, to see Georgia bite her lips so as not to smile in an *I told you so* sort of way.

"So then, Sir Francis's death has been solved?" she ventured. "Pardon my candor—of course you may not be at liberty to tell me."

"*Si*, we believe it has. It was not an accident, Signorina, but the result of an assassination."

"*What?*"

Georgia poked her. "What did he say?"

She translated, and watched her companion's face go as slack with horror as her own.

"But—but—" Millie got her racing mind under control with difficulty. "Can you tell me how your excellent police force arrived at this conclusion? It seems … extraordinary." *Unbelievable* was the word she would have used had she not been sure it would offend them.

Short gazed at her sorrowfully. "*La Serenissima* is the most beautiful city in the Levant, but it does have its failings. And one of those is the presence of the criminal element. Assassins may be hired by anyone who can pay their fee. In most cases, these are invisible to tourists such as yourself, but sometimes their actions do intrude upon the lives of the innocent."

I should say so. "And you believe Sir Francis—"

The rotund man nodded. "As a diplomat, he has been a known proponent of technology to better the lives of our citizens. There are those who do not approve. Our investigations are, of course, ongoing, but it is more than possible one such person hired an assassin to bring progress in that direction to a halt."

"Good heavens," Georgia said, upon hearing the translation. "That's unbelievable."

Millie did not translate. Instead, she said, "I cannot tell you how much we appreciate the hard work you have devoted to the case. Thank you for coming to tell us in person. Are we—are we in any danger from this assassin?"

Long shook his head. "No, Signorina. His remit was to remove Sir Francis, and he has done so. It is doubtful that he is even aware of the consequences he has visited upon you. For which we convey our deep regret."

He bowed, and Short said, "Thank you for receiving us. We wish you a pleasant holiday and a safe return to England."

The ever-vigilant Signore Airone showed them out. It was a good thing, too, for Millie's knees would have failed her had she attempted to stand.

Silently, she met Georgia's incredulous gaze.

"Surely this is an elaborate prank," Millie said. "The word *assassin* could not possibly have crossed that man's lips."

"I have every confidence in your grasp of Italian." Georgia spoke in a dazed way, as though it was an effort to remember how.

"I would not have predicted *that* as a solution. I would sooner have put my money on a kraken. At least there is logic in it."

"Convenience trumps logic," Georgia said with a touch of bitterness. "It seems Mr Seacombe was right last night when he wondered why so much effort has gone into burying the investigation, not solving it."

"They are certainly grasping at straws. Assassins." Millie shook her head. "So where does that leave us? With a gondolier assassin, leaving his handiwork in plain view and strolling up the canal to vanish?"

Georgia turned to look at the French doors that opened on the balcony where they had breakfasted. "Did he vanish, though? How many people *do* wade in the canals here?"

"I certainly have not seen any. Even the sight of a baby kraken would be enough to dissuade me." Millie shuddered.

"He must have climbed out somewhere. If he did, he might have left evidence." Georgia turned back, her eyes bright with a new idea. "We have nothing to occupy ourselves with except painting. If you would like to continue your sketch, I shall not stop you. But I may just take a stroll along the canal. Even though the bridges went up, our side is still intact. There is a fifty percent chance he might have climbed out on this side."

"But Georgia, dearest, that was a week ago."

"You saw how the mud had dried on Mr Seacombe's steps."

"I did." Millie was able to stand perfectly well now. "The painting can wait. Let me get my hat."

CHAPTER ELEVEN

*T*eddy had been an active, inquisitive child, and his best friend at Langford Park had been Anthony, the estate manager's son. Consequently, mud and dirt had been as much a part of his person as hands or feet. Strolling along the *fondamente* above the canal, Georgia's gaze swept the slates, alert for its familiar, telltale presence. While it was a deep brownish black when wet, the mud of Venice dried to the shade of the pale clay she had noted on Mr Seacombe's steps.

It was unfortunate for their purposes that the inhabitants of villa and tenement took scrupulous care of their section of the *fondamente*. In the pools of shade, evidence of wash water that hadn't yet dried was visible.

"I am beginning to think my idea was not such a good one," Georgia murmured to Millie. "They likely wash or sweep the pavement every day, and all trace has probably been gone for a week."

"Let us continue a little longer. We must stop up there in

any case, where our canal meets another. There does not appear to be a bridge."

The reason for this was soon apparent. The shabby little canal that interrupted their progress looked more like access to a liquid alley further along, which ran behind the grander houses for the delivery of coal and food, out of sight of the public. It did not warrant a bridge, being solely for the use of boatmen. Once the right turn was made, the *fondamente* narrowed from the usual width of five or more feet to no more than eighteen inches, broken only by doors and inlets for deliveries.

"Bother," Georgia sighed. They stood together at the corner, disappointed. "He must have climbed out on the other side."

"Goodness knows where that neighborhood is now."

"How maddening." She peered down the little canal. "Wait —does that look like mud? There, where you can see an iron ring set into the wall?"

"I can see the ring, but your eyesight is better than mine." Millie gazed at her in alarm. "You are not going to try to walk that narrow bit, are you?"

"I have crossed the trout stream at Langford Park on a fallen log. This at least is flat."

"But Georgia, what if you fall in?"

"You must haul me out, I suppose. It cannot be deep, if our gondolier walked all the way up here."

"If that mud is indeed evidence of such a thing, and not merely a place where a bag of foodstuffs was unloaded."

Georgia did not point out that a bag of foodstuffs was not likely to have been dunked in mud on its journey to some-one's table. She was busy unlacing her half-boots. "I must satisfy myself we have done our best. Here, take my boots. If I do fall in, I should regret ruining them. Luckily this is not one of my good skirts."

She edged her way out onto the narrow *fondamente*, facing the water, her posterior brushing the plaster wall. One could not walk along it in the normal fashion—particularly if one were in possession of hips. Out of the sun, the slates were cool on her stockinged feet. She had only about twenty feet to traverse, doing her best to keep her eyes on the pavement ahead and not on the gentle ripples in the water below.

The ripples were not caused by the passage of krakens. Certainly not. It was simply the natural movement of the slow current between buildings.

Breathing deeply, she reached her goal, where indeed a splotch of mud had dried on the slates. A splotch not in the least like footprints. In fact, it did rather look as though a bag of something had been set here.

Since she was alone, she had the satisfaction of using an epithet not suitable for company. There was nothing for it but to edge her way back and admit defeat.

She turned, hands flat on the plaster, toes curling over the edge of the pavement.

Something rolled under the surface of the water, and— dear heaven, was that a *tentacle*?

Something like a whimper came out of her throat. Did it see her? Her toes—would it wrap around her toes? She tried to pull them in—*no room—don't overbalance—oh no—no!*

Arms flailing, Georgia lost her footing, tipped off the narrow pavement and plunged feet first into the canal.

Was that a scream? No, it was herself, wailing incoher-ently, thigh-deep in water, her nearly bare feet sinking into the horrid mud up over her ankles. Bubbles burst on the surface and released puffs of fetid air.

The kraken rolled to the surface as it passed her billowing linen skirts—*heaven help me*—

It was a clump of seaweed.

"You ridiculous fool," she gasped, "you've sacrificed a pair of stockings and any semblance of dignity you ever possessed."

At least she'd landed right way up. She craned her neck, trying to see Millie up on the *fondamente* at the intersection of the canals, but she was nowhere in sight.

Where had she gone? And more important, how was one to get out?

And then she spotted an iron ladder, just a little way past the splotch of mud. There was no option—she must slog down there and haul herself out. Grimacing in distaste at what her feet might be encountering in the mud, she waded back the way she had come, hoping to goodness there was no broken glass buried beneath, and that no gondolier would round the corner and run her down, unable to see her from the stern of his long hull.

Venice had far too many perils. What had possessed her to suggest to Teddy that it would be a good place for a painting holiday?

At the ladder, she flung her sopping skirts over one shoulder—what did it matter, her blouse was soaked—and climbed out of the canal. As her eyes came level with the pavement, she saw that she was not the only one to have used this ladder, which could not be seen from above.

There were footprints dried on the slates. Not just here, for as she climbed out, water streamed from her clothes and washed away the mud she'd brought with her. But a few feet along, there they were.

She wrung out her skirts in a cascade and held them up behind her as she bent to look.

How very odd. She felt quite free to believe these prints belonged to the murderous gondolier, for who else would be climbing out of a canal this close to the scene of a crime? The soles of his shoes had a chevron pattern. She'd never seen that before—leather soles tended to be smooth. At the ball of the foot was a circle. A maker's mark? Some indication of livery? Whatever design had been in the small circle was simply a dried glob now.

But as he walked, perhaps some of the mud would wear away and she could see the design. Two prints. Three. She followed them, careful every moment not to overbalance.

Oh dear. They were fading now. She bent to examine the last clear-ish one. Inside the circle—was that a number? Eleven? Seventeen? It could even be a fourteen.

Bother.

Well, there was still something she could do. She extended her own foot and placed it inside the print. Wider. And longer by at least three inches. She committed her foot, the print, and its patterns to memory. As soon as she got back to the villa, she would draw it in her sketchbook and show it to Mr Seacombe. He would likely find the whole escapade amusing, but—

"Georgia!"

Cautiously, she turned on the narrow pavement to see Lorenzo in his gondola, steering Millie toward her significantly faster than was his usual wont. Georgia retraced her steps back to the iron ladder.

"Are you all right?"

"Yes. I am unhurt."

Lorenzo slowed the gondola to bring it level with where she stood.

"Oh, my dear, what a sight you are!"

"Never mind me—look! I have found footprints. Lorenzo, come tell me what you make of these."

"But Signora, you will catch a chill."

"Bother that. Come and look."

Obligingly, he placed a foot on the iron ladder to hold the vessel steady. He peered over the lip of the pavement, and grinned, his teeth showing very white in his tanned, hand-some face. "Those are a gondolier's shoes, with rubber soles. Had anyone seen him, he would never have—how do you say?" From his perch at the stern, he looked down at Millie, seated on the cushioned bench and gripping the gunwales with a hand on either side.

"Lived it down?"

"*Si*. It is a great shame to fall in. Not only because of the krakens. A good boatman should have more than just knowl-edge of the canals. He must have both balance and foresight. To fall in, one loses the reputation for both."

"You have both," Georgia said, quite truthfully. She had great respect for Lorenzo's foresight.

"*Si*, Signora," he agreed.

"What else can you tell us about these prints, Lorenzo? For I think they may have been made by the man who killed Sir Francis."

"Signorina Brunel has already told me why you were out this afternoon. May I ask that you look at my shoes?"

He held up the foot on the ladder, and Georgia and Millie both craned to look.

"It is a different pattern," Georgia said. "A square lattice. These prints are chevrons."

He practiced the new word. "*Si*. That signifies the shoemaker. The shoes with the *chevron* are made by Giorgio Petrale, in San Polo."

"And this circle?"

"That identifies the boatman for whom they are made."

"Is there nothing you do not know?" Georgia said with frank admiration.

"You are kind, Signora. I am ignorant of much in this world, because I am young, but Venice and the art of the gondola? Of that I know much."

"Will you take us to see Signore Petrale?"

Millie shook her head. "Georgia, dear, I think he had better take you home to change."

Georgia opened her mouth to protest, but Lorenzo forestalled her.

"His shop is not open now—it is the siesta. We will go in the morning, when there are fewer customers. Nine o'clock. And now, Signora, please step down into the gondola. I must convey you home before anyone sees you."

At the villa, Lorenzo's grandmother raised her eyebrows at the state of her ladyship's clothes, but assured her that her skirt, petticoats, and blouse could all be laundered to a fine semblance of their original state. The stockings, sadly, were a lost cause, being both torn and black to the ankle.

Bathed and dressed in a voile tea gown of pale green embroidered with damask roses and trimmed with one of her new lace collars, Georgia settled at the sitting-room table to sketch what she had seen. She began with an outline of her own foot on the page, then drew the gondolier's shoe shape around it. A second drawing showed the chevron pattern and the circle, and the fact that the rubber-soled shoes appeared to have no heels.

"I have no idea what help all this will be, or even if the owner of these shoes has any connection with poor Sir Francis," she said to Millie, who was watching. "But I am not about to put his death down to some nameless assassin, either."

"Far too convenient," Millie agreed. "They said the investigation was ongoing, but you may be sure *we* have heard the end of it."

"I am half tempted to have a word with Sir Ernest, and ask him to hound them regularly for progress reports. How is Sir Francis, a diplomat in Her Majesty's service, to be treated so shabbily?"

"Perhaps you ought to wait, dear. Sir Ernest has been employed enough on our behalf, in causing them to cease hounding *you*."

She had a point.

"I am sure he knows his duty, and will do what is right." Georgia closed the sketchbook and put the pencils back in their case. "We are expected at the Seacombe house for dinner Friday evening. After we visit Signore Petrale the shoemaker, I hope we will have something worthwhile to share."

"I wonder if Mr Seacombe gleaned anything further from the monks?"

There was that, too.

Conversation at the dinner table was likely to be lively. And it would show Cora that some, at least, cared whether or not her father's murderer was ever brought to justice.

Thursday, May 9, 1895

At nine o'clock, Lorenzo was waiting at the water stairs to convey Georgia and Millie to Signore Petrale, the shoemaker. When they arrived at his shop in the Dorsoduro, Lorenzo performed the necessary introductions, after which Millie took Georgia's sketchbook from her and opened it on the counter.

"We are trying to locate the man for whom you made these shoes, Signore," she said. He was perhaps ten years older than Millie herself, and had a twinkle in his eye that boded well.

"How well our language sounds upon your tongue, Signorina," he said.

Goodness. Millie could feel the heat rising in her cheeks, which only made him smile more broadly. *"Grazie, Signore."*

"But why should you be trying to locate them? Do you wish to hire a gondolier? Is this young rascal here not suitable?"

"He is indeed most suitable. But a man wearing these shoes performed a unique service for us the other day and then disappeared before we could thank him. We should dearly like to call upon him and give him our thanks in person." She allowed one hand to caress the velvet of her reticule.

He nodded with satisfaction, all further questions answered by the unspoken. Peering at the sketchbook's pages, he murmured, "A size nine. Very common. But the customer number, I am desolated to say, is blocked out."

"It was an eleven, a seventeen, or possibly a fourteen," Millie said. "We had only footprints to go by, and not in good condition."

"Ah. Then we are down to three men. May I?"

He produced a pen, and in careful, beautifully shaped script, wrote three names and addresses on the page. Lorenzo leaned in. "I can find them, Signorina."

Millie thanked Signore Petrale, and wondered if it would be gauche to offer him payment for his information. Then she had an idea. "Signore, do you keep shoes in reserve for the gondoliers, so that they do not have to wait for a new pair?"

"I do indeed, Signorina."

"You are a prudent businessman, I see. Then, may I purchase a pair for dear Lorenzo? He and you have been of inestimable service to us."

"Signorina!" Lorenzo protested. "I cannot— I will not hear of—"

He could and he must.

"You are generosity itself." Signore Petrale bowed. "I shall return in a moment."

Over Lorenzo's ongoing protests, she neatly accomplished two tasks in one and left the shop with bows and smiles. Dear Lorenzo was worth his weight in gold. A new pair of shoes was the least she could do, after all his many services.

Which were not yet concluded this morning. They visited the first two addresses, to discover that gondoliers numbered eleven and fourteen had been home by midnight on the night of the king and queen's ball, having conveyed their fares there and gone home.

Number seventeen was their last hope. Millie's stomach was slightly wobbly with nerves as Lorenzo poled the gondola to a stop outside a tenement that housed several families. Its plaster was patchy with age, but the pavement in front had been scrubbed. In the tiny courtyard, off of which half a dozen doors opened, a staircase ran up to a veranda where washing hung. Lorenzo inquired of a child bouncing a ball against the wall, and they gathered outside the door on the ground level to which he had pointed.

A wreath of dried grapevine hung upon it, black ribbons twisted around it to terminate in a large, drooping bow.

Lorenzo knocked, and in a moment, a tired-looking woman opened the door, a baby on her hip. She was dressed entirely in black.

"*Sì?*"

Millie had a moment to be thankful that Lorenzo was with them. Rapidly, he introduced himself and his ladies and told their story—that number seventeen, Signore Bruno, had performed a great service in pulling her ladyship from a canal, and they wished to thank him in person now that her ladyship was recovered.

Oh, Lorenzo was good. Shoes were not sufficient. Millie made a mental note to set aside some coins for him before they departed Venice.

The woman's gaze moved from Georgia to Millie and back to Lorenzo. "I am afraid they are too late," she said in the Veneziano accent that was so difficult to understand. "My husband is dead."

Morto. That was clear enough.

Millie could not stop herself. "What has happened, my dear Signora?"

The woman looked surprised at her command of the language, and switched to Italian. "It happened after the king and queen's ball. He worked nearly all that night, ferrying people around the city. There were so many gondoliers in the canals that his own was struck by some reckless fool, and for the first time, he fell into the water."

Lorenzo made a sound, half commiseration, half surprise.

"There was a kraken," Signora Bruno said sadly. "The canal was in complete chaos. His gondola was gone by the time he found a place to climb out. And then, on his way to Signore Barcaiolo's boatyard the next day to see if it had turned up, he —he—" She choked.

Millie fished a handkerchief out of her reticule and handed it to her. The woman wiped her tears and blew her nose. She offered the scrap of cambric to Millie, who folded her fingers around it. "Keep it, Signora. What happened on the way to the boatyard?"

"It was before dinner. Nearly dark. And—and he was stabbed, Signorina. The criminals from Napoli, of course, here for easy pickings at the exhibition. The night watch found him in a doorway, dead an hour already, as they began their rounds."

Millie translated rapidly for Georgia, whose eyes widened in horror as she raised a hand to her lips.

"Our deepest condolences upon your loss," Millie said. "I hope you will do us the honor of accepting the gift we brought for your husband."

She and Georgia emptied their pocketbooks. It was too late to pay for the funeral, but the equivalent of ten pounds in Italian coin might, at least, keep the widow and her children in food for a little while. Then they took their leave.

It was not until they were on their way, Lorenzo at the helm in the labyrinth of canals, that Millie glanced up at him. "What are your thoughts on this matter, Lorenzo?"

"I think that, kraken or not, no respectable gondolier would leave his only means of income floating in the canal while he went home to bed," Lorenzo said. "There was no accident."

"He abandoned it at our water stairs," Georgia agreed. "And made up a grand tale for his poor wife."

"*Si.*" Lorenzo seemed to be creating the scenario in his mind as he steered down a long canal. "He was hired to convey Sir Francis away from the ball, and to kill him. I will lay a year's wages on it, Signora. He left the oar and the gondola at the villa so they could not be connected with him, but with you. He walked up the canal and climbed out, then returned home, suitably muddy and wet, with the story."

"Only to be set upon the next day by a criminal from Napoli." Millie shook her head. "Thus relieving the party who hired him of the obligation to pay him."

"I do not think we may malign the people of Napoli so readily." Georgia waited for a gondola with a curtained cabin to pass them. "I have no proof to back it up, but what if Signore Bruno was eliminated by an assassin to prevent his ever telling the true tale?"

"Tying—how do you say?" Lorenzo asked. "The bow?"

"Tying up loose ends," Millie supplied. "I suppose we will never know, but there is as good a chance of that, I suppose, as there is of its being a Napolitan footpad here for the exhibition."

"Assassins are blamed for everything in Venice, it seems," Georgia observed.

"There is no shortage of them, Signora," Lorenzo said. "Do not discount them. They are very real. There are certain families whose names I would not speak aloud in public. But even I do not believe there can be such a coincidence as this. A gondolier kills a man and is stabbed to death himself not a day later? The two events connect themselves in my mind."

He turned a corner by pushing off a wall with one foot, and they were in their own familiar canal. The cheerful yellow plaster of the Villa dei Pappagalli looked positively welcoming on a morning that had been so difficult.

Difficult, and sad, and disappointing.

Millie found it a great pity that one could not drink the fine Umbrian port until after dinner.

CHAPTER TWELVE

FRIDAY, MAY 10, 1895 AT 2:00 A.M

*G*eorgia woke with a start. A cold, strong hand was pressed to her mouth so tightly she could not even part her lips enough to bite.

She attempted to scream, but only a thready squeak came out, like a frightened mouse.

"Do not make a sound, I beg you." The whisper came out of the dark.

An assassin!

Georgia froze. Even her blood seemed to halt in her veins.

"I mean you no harm, Lady Langford. I have only come for Cora."

You and at least three others. Well, you shall not have her.

"If I release you, will you promise not to scream?"

Georgia nodded. She held the scream in reserve.

The hand slid away, and the weight of a body lifted from her mattress. "I will light a lamp, so we may speak like civilized people."

Georgia checked herself in the act of rolling to the other

side of the bed to flee. What kind of assassin lit a lamp and allowed you to see his face?

The kind who planned to kill you after his *civilized conversation*, that was who.

The lamp flared into life, and the assassin's black silhouette moved aside, considerately turning into its illumination.

Georgia's limbs went liquid with shock as she recognized the face from the daguerreotype beside Cora's bed.

"Lady Thorne?" She flopped back into her pillows. "Was this entirely necessary?"

"I'm afraid so." The low voice was filled with regret. "I do apologize, but it is absolutely vital that no one knows I am in Venice. Where is Cora?"

"She is not here." Georgia gathered herself together enough to swing her feet down and sit on the side of her bed while her nocturnal guest took the wing chair near the lamp.

"Yes, I have ascertained that already. I have searched the house and found neither her nor her traveling closet. I do hope you will explain."

"I think we both have quite a lot to explain." Georgia's heart was slowing from a panicked gallop to a refreshing trot. "But first things first—Cora is safe. She is with trusted friends. You are, I believe, acquainted with Cornelius van Meere?"

Lady Thorne straightened in surprise. "Yes. But what—?"

"He is in Venice for a series of meetings with the government. But he is not relevant. His bodyguard, Mr Dustin Seacombe, is at present Cora's host. She became friends with his son Marcus during the second kidnapping attempt."

"There have been two?"

"Three, I am sad to say. The night before the art exhibition opened, Cora woke to find a man in her room. She hid, and evaded him. Then, the Minister of Public Works, Arturo del Campo, asked me to hand Cora over into his keeping. Since the second attempt happened as he was making his offer, I count his as number three."

"In that you are mistaken, Lady Langford. It is number four."

Georgia stared. "Good heavens. That poor child. When was the fourth?"

"It is actually the first. When her father brought her to Venice."

Several facts in Georgia's memory rearranged themselves to create a new picture. "'It was supposed to be a grand adventure,'" she breathed. "That is what Cora said. I could not understand how she could be removed from school ... why there was no staff but for the cook and majordomo ... why she would spy on her father and his guests for amusement, not do the normal things children do when on holiday."

"Not amusement." Lady Thorne smiled, and her finely sculpted, no-nonsense face blossomed into humor and beauty. "Practice."

"She really is a very good spy," Georgia confided. "I hope her education takes that into account."

"If we both survive this, that is my int—"

The door opened, and a fireplace poker slid into the room. Millie was right behind it, eyes wide with fear. "Georgia?"

"It is all right, Millie," she said. "This is Lady Thorne, Cora's mother."

The poker lowered suddenly enough for its tip to bounce off the plank floor, its handle loose in fingers relaxed with shock.

Lady Thorne rose and offered her hand. "Do call me Louise, both of you. This is no time to stand on ceremony."

"I should say not, since two of us are in nightgowns," Millie managed. She laid the poker on the floor in order to shake Louise Thorne's hand. Then she closed the door and joined Georgia on the edge of the bed. She peered at their guest. "I am Millicent Brunel. Lady Langford is my late nephew's wife. I say, are those ... bloomers?"

Louise looked down as though to remind herself what she was wearing. "They are. One cannot very well cycle down out of the Alps in skirts. Or scale walls, for that matter."

After a moment of unsuccessfully trying to make sense of this, Georgia said, "Perhaps you might begin at the beginning, Louise. And with your mind now at ease concerning Cora, we will add our part of the story."

Louise nodded. "A sensible plan. Very well."

"One moment. I will be right back." Georgia slipped downstairs to the sitting room, collected the port decanter and three short stemmed glasses, and brought them back into her bedchamber.

Louise smiled as she toasted Georgia with her filled glass. "You are a queen among women. As I said, Francis took Cora without my knowledge on his last conjugal visit to Munich. She has told you of my work there?"

Georgia took a sip of the fine vintage and nodded. "A very little. You are an engineer of some repute, I understand."

"And all these troubles seem to revolve around a breakwater?" Millie added.

Louise looked surprised. "How very clever of you to deduce that. I am at present designing one to be installed just off the shores of the city of Nouveau Orléans. The one I designed in Flanders is now operational, though its purpose is different. The first is to keep the sea from inundating the city. The second is so that the Flemish may begin reclaiming land."

"And what of the one here?" Georgia asked. "Cora tells us that Sir Francis met several times with del Campo and the Conte di Narbone's cousin Alessandro to discuss it."

Louise leaned back in the comfortable chair with her port. "That is the sticking point. Discussions were indeed ongoing. But when I discovered quite by accident the actual purpose of the breakwater, I refused to go further and withdrew from the scheme."

Georgia didn't know which question to ask first.

"The actual purpose?" Millie prompted.

"They wish to build it out there in the lagoon under the auspices of public works. To control the *acqua alta*—the waters that flood the city when the high tides and heavy rains of winter combine."

"But that is not its purpose?" Georgia could not imagine what else one would do with a breakwater.

"Have you a pencil and paper?"

Wordlessly, Georgia fetched her sketchbook and pencil case, and opened the former to a fresh page.

"Here is Venice in its traditional configuration. Here are the islands in the lagoon." The pencil *skritch*ed in the silence. "And here are the proposed breakwaters, from island to island."

"It looks like a moat," Georgia said.

"Exactly. And what is the purpose of a moat?"

"To keep one's enemies out," Millie said. "And for swans."

"Indeed. And who are the Doge's enemies?"

Georgia thought for a moment. "Why, no one. Venice has

had no enemies since the fifteenth century, when the gear-works became operational and the city took back all the pros-perity it had begun to lose."

"Exactly. No enemies but the one the present Doge cannot fight—himself. He is determined to be king, you see. And if he walls Venice off, Italy loses its only port in the Levant. Its gateway for transport of its goods into the countries east of here, and of the riches that consequently flow to it. With Venice an armed castle, King Umberto will be forced to allow him to secede and declare himself king. And all the work of unification will be undone."

Georgia and Millie were silent, taking this in. How utterly mad.

"Imagine the expense," was all Georgia could think of to say.

"And the destruction of lagoon and islands," Millie added. "And the time—my goodness, the man will be dead before he can place a crown on his head."

"Not so," Louise said. "Flanders constructed theirs—only half the size, mind you, and minus the requirement for heavy artillery—in two years."

"Heavy artillery?" Georgia repeated.

"Oh, yes. The list of requirements I was not supposed to see included cannon on each section of the breakwater."

"You were not supposed to see—what? Who may conceal anything from you, the designer?" Millie asked.

Louise shook her head. "Francis. He is a born diplomat, skilled at persuasion and convincing people who hate each other to work together. That's why he was posted here. But a man of organization and attention to detail he is not. Cora was drawing on the back of a large piece of paper, and when I went in to kiss her good night, there it was, written out on the other side, with preliminary drawings. The Doge's actual requirements for the mechanical substructure."

"I can hardly take it in," Georgia said. "But I suppose the most important question is, what has this to do with Cora?"

"Well may you ask. May I pour us all a refill?"

"Only one," Millie warned. "This port comes from our signora's family in Umbria. It will lay you out."

"Noted." Louise poured efficiently, without spilling a tawny drop. She took a sip, as though organizing her thoughts. "I confronted Francis and he told me all. The next thing I knew, his conjugal leave had been abruptly rescinded. Sir Ernest needed him urgently. He departed while I was attending the Empress at the Linderhof. It was not until I returned the following day that I discovered he had taken Cora with him. By then it was too late. They had already landed in Venice and Cora wrote with great excitement about the villa and the chickens. I did not know, then, that my husband was acting under duress—upon instructions from Minister del Campo."

"Instructions to remove his own child from her mother?" Georgia said incredulously. "But why?"

"Insurance, I suspect. Control."

"But why murder him if he had done as intructed?" Millie wanted to know. "Del Campo had seen her himself at their villa."

"He had been useful, but I was not flying immediately to his side to retrieve my child." Louise's face was averted. "Had I done so, had I not been so focused on completing the Empress's plaything, my husband might still be alive."

"And you would have been forced to create what amounts to a massive weapon of war," Georgia said.

"I could have," Louise said simply. "I could have created the design, received a handsome sum for it, and retired with Francis and Cora to my family's estate in Kent."

"And you would have been as great a monster as the Doge, or del Campo," Millie breathed. "Heaven save them from a woman of substance and character."

"I am quite certain that is not how the Doge would have put it." Louise's lips quirked in a rueful smile. "In any case, they were forced to raise the stakes. Or perhaps Francis protested the use of his family in this way. I will never know. He was murdered, and that left Cora alone in Venice—the lure I would not be able to resist."

"Except that we got there before del Campo or the police did," Georgia said on a note of realization. "We removed her that very morning, following the failure of a housebreaker to find her mere hours before."

Millie thought out loud. "Sir Francis was left floating at our water stairs. The *polizia* arrived that same morning and said we could not leave Venice. They said it was because Georgia was a suspect."

"For the crime of dancing with him," Georgia said bitterly.

"But it was really to immobilize us until they could discover what we had done with Cora. Which they did, since, all unsuspecting, we went about Venice with her in broad daylight," Millie said. "It was only a matter of waiting for the right moment. Had she not been the resourceful child she is, with a brave and capable friend in Marcus, I shudder to think how they might have used her."

Rapidly, Georgia explained to Lady Thorne about the

funeral, the spice chest, and the children's flight through the canals and lanes of Venice. "I can only be thankful they did not meet with a kraken," she concluded. "How would I be able to break the news of your child's death to you, who have already endured that of your husband?"

"There is nothing to dread in the krakens," Louise said, overlooking the reference to her husband and speaking in the same tone in which one might refer to a feisty rooster. "They are exceedingly intelligent. One of my colleagues wrote her doctoral thesis on their ability to transfer thoughts among themselves using electrical impulses. It is fascinating—they create a kind of field around themselves in which to communicate. What she did not expect to discover is that this communication extends to other species. Fish. Octopuses. And humans."

Having never seen a kraken outside of the pages of a novel, Georgia's ability to imagine krakens talking to each other fell a little short. "Then ... do you mean to say ... if the people sentenced to die cleaning the gearworks simply took the time to listen to the krakens' thoughts, they would be permitted by the creatures to escape?"

"Remarkable, is it not? You would think people would at least read a treatise. It was published widely in Bavaria."

But not, presumably, in Venice, where it would be used to help condemned prisoners escape and render the punishment obsolete.

"They are imprisoned, not by the krakens, but by their own fear," Millie said in a wondering tone. "Imagine the civilization Venice might have had if they had only listened to the creatures."

"The krakens are perfectly capable of making their own

145

moat," Louise agreed. "The breakwater is unnecessary. But the construction of it will probably hurt so many of them that the poor beings will do nothing but attack."

Georgia shuddered. "Let us return to our situation. It is more than dire enough for me. At what point did you go missing?"

"When I received your cable." Louise smiled at her. "Forgive me—I sent the reply using dear Herr Brucker's name, and departed forthwith on a cycling tour."

Georgia and Millie stared at her, then at the bloomers. Then back up to her dancing eyes.

"I could not travel by conventional methods, of course," she explained. "Francis had taken our personal airship, and a public vessel would have been stopped and searched the moment it landed. The trains likewise. The roads through the mountains were as yet impassable so early in the year, so my steam landau was out of the question. That left one option—I became Maria Brucker, booked myself on a tour departing Munich the next day, and packed a rucksack with a few necessities."

"You cycled over the Alps? Snow and glaciers notwithstanding?" Millie's voice was hushed with admiration.

"No indeed. Heavens above. The tour took us over the mountains themselves in a private airship. We disembarked north of Lago Garda, were issued a steamcycle each, and rolled away." She smiled, all mischief and sparkle. "Really, it is a lovely method of travel. Cycle all day and a comfortable bed in a *pension* each night. We arrived at the station this evening, turned in our cycles, and I simply melted into the crowd to board a vaporetto. I knew your villa's name, and had merely to be conveyed here. After that I confess I scaled the side of the building. I hope you do not mind terribly. It was a bit tricky with the full moon."

"Not at all. My hat is off to you." Having no hat, or nightcap either, Georgia bowed.

Millie leaned limply on the bedpost. "I am quite breathless, and that is without cycling. My word, Louise, you are a heroine."

"No," she said modestly. "I am a mother and an engineer. Nothing more."

"We must see you reunited with your daughter with all possible speed," Georgia said, recovering from these revelations with difficulty. "It is not safe for you to stay here. Our enemies will discover, if they have not already, that Cora is not here, and then goodness knows what will happen."

"Lorenzo can take Louise to Mr Seacombe quietly," Millie said.

Georgia tilted her head. "That he can. Along with you, Millie. To dinner this evening, in fact. Even the most persistent pair of eyes will see nothing but two ladies leaving the villa, as they do daily. Louise can wear some of my clothes and a veiled hat."

"And you?" Louise's brow pleated with concern.

"I shall stay here." It was better that congenial evenings with Mr Seacombe were kept to a minimum, in any case. "Any third lady will give the game away."

"But Georgia—"

"She is right," Louise said reluctantly. "There cannot be three ladies. Once Cora and I are reunited, we will disappear. Millie will come home, and no one will be the wiser."

Millie did not look pleased with Georgia's part of this

plan. "Now is not the time to leave you alone in the house, dearest."

"I shall be quite safe," Georgia assured her. "Signore Airone's family is here, and now I have a fireplace poker to arm myself with."

"You are mocking me," Millie said severely.

"I adore you." She squeezed her about the waist. "Louise, I would not put you in the macaw's room for anything, but you are very welcome to sleep in Cora's. The parakeets will be happy to watch over your rest."

"Thank you. I accept. Until morning, then."

Until morning.

And after that, Louise and Cora might cycle out of her life, and she would never see either one again.

Somehow, this idea was much more distressing than Georgia had expected.

CHAPTER THIRTEEN

10:15 A.M.

*T*he ladies of the villa slept late. Upon waking, Georgia ordered a particularly large breakfast, which Signora Airone was only too delighted to provide. She believed that Millie needed fattening up, so the trays laid upon the table out on the balcony included omelettes, roast potatoes, and both muffins and scones, along with pots of butter and jam. Millie quietly conveyed a third of everything to the parakeets' room, and just as quietly fetched the empty dishes back again.

"You must not betray your presence here," she whispered to Lady Thorne as she departed. "But if the signora should take it into her head to clean this room, I do not know how to prevent it."

"The windows are large, and face the back," Louise whispered back. "Should it be necessary, I shall climb out and sun myself on the roof until she is gone. Do not worry."

Easier said than done. When had anyone ever been able to conceal anything from the staff?

But they managed it, and stayed quietly indoors, getting

better acquainted with Louise Thorne and doing their best to curb her impatience for the evening to come.

At last, as the sun set, Louise turned from Georgia's cheval glass and presented herself to the two of them for inspection. "Will I do?"

She was only an inch or two shorter than Georgia, and her figure was not quite so fashionable, being wiry and strong enough to scale the sides of villas. Millie had no doubt this was the result of dragging gears and engines about in laboratories. But it was easily solved. Louise wore her own bloomers beneath Georgia's navy linen walking skirt, with a wide belt to cinch in the waist, and the waistband turned over once to bring up the hem. Her boots were her own, and her blouse under the matching jacket with its broad Brussels lace collar concealed her figure. With the veil of Georgia's navy straw hat drawn down below her chin, and her hair dressed high and full instead of in a practical braided bun at her nape, even Millie would have mistaken her for Georgia in the street.

"Yes," Millie said. "You will do."

"You will both be careful," Georgia said anxiously. "Please ask Mr Seacombe to escort you back afterward."

"Georgia, do not fret," Millie said. "Lorenzo is taking us both ways, remember?"

She took a deep breath. "Yes, of course. What was I thinking?"

"The habits of London are deeply ingrained," Louise said kindly. "I remember declining a carriage in order to get in a brisk walk home. My dears, may we be off? I am more anxious to see Cora than you can imagine."

"Good heavens," Millie said. "Of course. Let us go at once."

Lorenzo steered them smoothly to the public jetty at the

Ponte Rialto, and from there both he and Millie were hard put to keep up with Louise. She looked over her shoulder only to receive directions, and was the first to bang imperiously on the sturdy blue door that concealed the presence of Mr van Meere from the world.

When they were admitted, she lifted the veil and gazed anxiously about the courtyard within.

"Mama!" came a cry from above, where two children were sitting on the stairs.

Cora flew down the steps as though airborne, and into her mother's arms. Millie's lips only trembled a little as Cora began to cry—at the half-gasped sentences directed into each other's hair—at the way Louise knelt, her arms wrapped around her daughter as though she would never let her go.

The door on the opposite side opened and a large personage who must be Mr van Meere peered out. Not recognizing anyone, he withdrew and banged the door shut, leaving Millie with an impression of dour impatience at being thus interrupted.

Marcus sat on a step about halfway down and grinned at Millie. "How did you find her?"

"She found us. Frightened us half to death in the middle of the night— Lady Langford thought it was an assassin."

"It could have been," the boy said wisely. "But I'm glad it wasn't."

Cora dried her tears with the hem of her pinafore. "You must come and meet Marcus, Mama. He is my friend."

Louise reached up to offer her hand to the boy, who hesitated, as though he thought she might expect it to be kissed. Then he decided to shake it. "How do, Lady Thorne?"

"Marcus," came a growl from above. "You know better than that."

The boy released her hand and descended to the courtyard. He cleared his throat and tried again. "How do you do, Lady Thorne? I am honored to make your acquaintance." He bowed.

"The honor is entirely mine, Master Seacombe. Oh, dash it all, come here. I want to hug you."

Marcus was engulfed in a hug, his eyes bugging out at the strength of it. Cora, clearly, was used to being in her mother's arms, but had not thought to warn her friend. By the time he emerged, red-faced, his father had descended and Millie recalled herself to her duties.

"Lady Louise Thorne, may I present Dustin Seacombe, of the Texican Rangers."

"Lady Thorne. Welcome to our home." He did kiss her hand, and somehow it looked utterly appropriate—or it would have seemed so, had Millie not seen the flush that burned into her cheeks. Goodness, the effect this man had on women!

When Louise reclaimed her hand, she said, "I owe you a debt I can never repay, Mr Seacombe. Thank you for keeping my daughter safe."

"No thanks necessary, ma'am. She's a pleasure to have around. Keeps my boy on his toes."

"We shall not trespass on your hospitality much longer, I trust."

"As long as you need, ma'am." He glanced at the staircase opposite. "I believe you know my employer?"

"I would not say I know him, but we are acquainted. He visited late last year, and spent some time in my laboratory. I should prefer, however, that he not know I am here. Should he inquire, Lady Langford came to call."

"Understood. Let's go up. The signora should have dinner ready soon. Lorenzo, will you join us?"

"No, Signore. I will dine with the signora's family. Her son David is my friend."

Mr Seacombe escorted Millie up the stairs and soon they were gathered around the table, where steaming plates of pasta were followed by medallions of pork and roasted vegetables. Louise regaled their hosts with the tale of her journey from Munich to Venice, which caused even Mr Seacombe to lay down his knife and fork to stare.

"By golly, ma'am, you are a wonder," he finally said.

"Georgia said something similar," Millie said with a smile. "But I would believe any woman of resources would have found a way to her child under such circumstances as these."

"You may be right," he said, shaking his head.

Cora looked pleased at having the credit of such a mother. "Shall we go home the same way, Mama?" she asked eagerly. "I could ride a steamcycle, I know I could."

"I have no doubt of that," Louise told her fondly. "But I believe we ought to take stock of our situation first. For you have an advantage that I did not."

Cora looked blank, her mind working furiously. Then her brow cleared. "The airship. Of course. We will simply go home in *Thetis*."

Mr Seacombe laid his knife and fork neatly on his empty plate. "The what now?"

"*Thetis*," Cora said. "We came here in her. She is a four-cabin Zeppelin with two Daimler engines."

"Nice," Marcus said. "We don't have an airship. We came with Mr van Meere."

"*Foresight* is substantially larger than *Thetis*," Louise said. "You would have been very comfortable for such a long voyage, though."

"It has its own island," Marcus confided. "It wouldn't fit on the Lido. We have to take a vaporetto out to it when we leave."

"Do you know when that will that be?" Millie asked.

"No, ma'am," Mr Seacombe said in a tone that gave her to understand he didn't want to say. Of course. His employer's movements were, in a word, secret.

"Is it safe for you to go back to Munich?" Marcus wanted to know. "Assassins can follow anybody if they've a mind to. Especially if they're Famiglia Rosa." His voice dropped to a whisper, as though someone might be listening outside the second-story window.

"What is that?" Millie asked, since no one else did.

"The worst of the assassins," Mr Seacombe said. "Run by the di Alba brothers in Venice, Naples, and Rome. Didn't happen to notice a gold medallion anywhere, did you?"

Millie shook her head. "Why?"

"It means they're under contract. And they won't stop until they achieve their objective, even if it takes years."

Millie felt the breath go out of her, and then did her best to rally. There had not, to her knowledge, been any medallion of any kind lying within sight since they had arrived in Venice.

"How do you propose to get to your ship, ma'am?" His attention turned back to Lady Thorne. "There might not be a medallion in play, but if Cora was to be used as bait to get you into Venice, they'll be watching for you. It won't be safe to go out to the Lido. They're likely expecting you to arrive there on the packet from Geneva."

"We can go at night," Cora suggested. "Can't we, Mama?"

"'Fraid that won't make much difference. Your ship will have been impounded. They'll want to make sure your escape is cut off."

"Impounded?" Louise echoed. "Then we shall simply scale the fence and be gone before they catch us."

"There's no fence, ma'am. Don't need it. Not with the guns."

Her wide green eyes held his gaze across the table. "Guns."

"Yep. Even Mr van Meere's vessel wouldn't survive lift, and it's got guns of its own."

Gracious. Millie had never heard of a private airship being armed. Perhaps it was a good thing it was moored on its own island.

"If I could make a suggestion … why don't you stay here?" Mr Seacombe pushed his plate aside and leaned on his elbows. "This is as close to a fortress as you'll get outside the Arsenale."

"She cannot stay here," Millie said crisply. Honestly, how like a man to suggest such a thing!

"Why not?" Cora said. "I want her to. Don't you want to stay, Mama?"

"I wish it above all things," Lady Thorne said simply, touching her daughter's cheek.

"That will not do," Millie told her. "Everyone outside this room—except Lorenzo—believes you to be Lady Langford. Need I explain the scandal it would cause if it were known you stayed here overnight? Or worse, for several nights?"

Louise Thorne's mouth opened, and after a moment, she

thought better of what she had been going to say, and closed it.

Mr Seacombe had absolutely no business looking as though he was enjoying the idea.

After a moment, he controlled himself, and his generous moustache ceased twitching as though he had been trying not to grin. "No one in Venice knows we're here except a very small number of people."

"Yes, well, one of those people is Arturo del Campo, and that is one too many," Millie retorted. "How long do you suppose it will be before he sends someone here to ask questions? After all, he saw you in our company on the balcony at the embassy."

"Not long," he agreed, readily enough to take the wind out of her sails. "Sounds like Lady Thorne and Cora might need to rejoin that cycling tour pronto, and skedaddle."

"Skedaddle!" Cora giggled. "Now, *that* is what *I* should wish above all things."

Millie was still thinking furiously. But until arrangements could be made, where could one hide a woman and child in Venice? A thousand places, no doubt, but where would be safest, and most unlikely to be searched by the authorities?

And then she had it.

"Mr van Meere's airship," she blurted. "How difficult would it be to hide Lady Thorne and Cora out there?"

A silence composed of astonishment and doubt fell like a curtain in the cheerful room.

Several seconds ticked by. "Difficult," Mr Seacombe said at last.

"Can you think of any other plan?"

"Steamcycles," Cora said, clearly unwilling to give them up.

"Risky, darling," her mother said. "I might have been able to pull it off once, but twice is tempting fate, I'm afraid. They will be watching for two of us."

"Do you speak Italian?" Mr Seacombe asked her.

Louise shook her head. "I cannot pose successfully as an Italian woman, if that is what you mean. I don't suppose French or German would be useful?"

"No." He gave a long, thoughtful sigh. "Seems we're at an impasse. I suppose I could ask. Or you could, since you're acquainted." He paused, frowning. "What gives me pause is the risk of one more person knowing you are here. Van Meere sees del Campo often enough that he could let something slip."

"Better to sneak them aboard *Foresight*," Marcus said, nodding. "The crew aren't aboard. I can't raise the gangway, but I can get in through the communications cage and let Cora and Lady Thorne in from inside. I've done it before."

"Sneaking is dishonorable," Millie objected. "It is trespassing."

"Not really," Marcus told her. "We came here on it, too, and—"

"Marcus."

The boy fell silent at his father's quiet rebuke.

"Let me think over how best to manage it," Mr Seacombe said. "I'll send a note by David in the morning. In the meantime, I hope you'll allow Cora to remain here."

It was very clear that this was the last thing Louise Thorne wanted, but in the end, she unwillingly gave in.

On the journey home, both of them once more veiled, Millie dared to speak in favor of the plan.

"There is a kind of sense, you know, in leaving her in a

house that has not yet been infiltrated," she said. "The police have been to our villa, and even you had no trouble getting in. Mr van Meere, you must agree, is living in the next thing to a fortress."

"I know it." Louise sighed. "But I am not required to like it."

"And we may be assured that Marcus will be with her every moment. I have the greatest confidence in Marcus."

"I do, too, oddly," Louise confessed with a little laugh. "Cora will not like being shut up in *Foresight*, but at least it is large enough to run races in, and presumably is well stocked. I would prefer to ask permission, but since that is not possible, I shall ask forgiveness instead. Thank goodness we are acquainted with Mr van Meere. I would never consider such a mad plan were it a stranger."

They fell silent for the rest of the journey. Mr Seacombe had promised to come up with a way to convey them to the moorage without attracting attention, but that did not stop Millie from running through possibilities herself.

And Georgia would have her own ideas, once they told her everything.

At the Villa dei Pappagalli, all lay dark and silent. A light glowed behind the door that led to the staff apartments and the kitchen. Millie and Louise climbed the stairs, and when they did not find Georgia in the sitting room, Millie said, "Surely she cannot have gone to bed. It is only nine, and she will be anxious to hear our news."

But she was not in her room. Millie lit a lamp and surveyed the neatly made bed and the nightdress laid across it.

"Perhaps she has gone up to the roof to enjoy the cool of the evening," Louise suggested.

"Neither of us have even attempted to find the way. We do not tend to enjoy roofs." Not after that incident with Hartford and the hunting rifle.

"She has been alone all evening," Louise pointed out. "I should do so. Let me run up there and check. Meanwhile, you ask the staff if she has gone out."

But Millie could not find anyone in the kitchen, and hesitated to invade Signore Airone's private quarters unless absolutely necessary. Lady Thorne returned to report that Georgia was not on the roof. Millie checked all the bedrooms, and even the macaw's closet, where the oar and Sir Francis's diary were—

Millie gasped, holding her lamp high. "Oh, dear heaven above." Her fingers went loose, and the lamp wobbled. "They're gone."

"What is? Something besides Georgia?"

"The oar—the murder weapon used to knock your husband unconscious, and to hold him under the water." So frightened was she that she forgot to cloak these appalling facts in gentler phrases. "And his appointment diary, containing evidence of his meetings with del Campo and others. Gone."

"Mr Seacombe was right." For the first time, the intrepid Louise Thorne sounded afraid.

Millie's hands shook, and the lamp's chimney chimed in its brass fittings before she could set it on the dresser. "They have taken Georgia. I know it. However are we to find her before it is too late?"

CHAPTER FOURTEEN

EARLIER THAT EVENING

Georgia had enjoyed a solitary dinner, doing her best not to feel sorry for herself. It was sure to be a merry party over at the Seacombes', and she would have loved to be there to see Cora's joyful reunion with her mother. But, she reflected over her gelato topped with fruit compôte, sometimes one must sacrifice one's own desires for the greater good.

Louise Thorne's safety was essential. There had been no other way to manage it but the way they had. And if said desires included seeing Dustin Seacombe again, well, they deserved to be sacrificed, also for the greater good.

She was curled up on the sitting-room sofa with a book about the history of Venice—in Italian, of course, but with spectacular plates—when Signore Airone appeared.

"The *polizia*, Signora. Are you at home?"

"What—now?" The mantel clock stood at five past eight.

"*Si*, Signora. Two officers we have not seen before, in the company of one Commissario Verdi. A man of greater rank than previously. It appears he has more questions."

"Good heavens. How inconvenient." She slid her feet back into her suede half-boots and did up the laces at speed. "Show him in, Signore. May I count upon you to translate?"

The man who was shown in was five or so years older than she, smooth of hair and wearing a beautifully cut suit. He bowed. "Good evening, Lady Langford. My deepest apologies for having interrupted you."

"Not at all." No need for translation, then. "Thank you, Signore Airone. Some tea, perhaps?" She turned to her visitor. "To what do I owe this visit, Commissario ... er ...?"

"Verdi." He held up a hand with a smile. "Yes, a distant relation of the composer, but with no talent along that line."

"Do be seated." She heard the sound of footsteps on the stairs. "Your men are joining us?"

"No indeed. They are carrying out their duties. We have a warrant to search the house."

Her blood froze in her veins. Cora's room—the oar—the appointment diary—

He twitched his trouser legs and seated himself in the armchair. "Allow me to get straight to the point. I understand from Minister del Campo that a young lady by the name of Cora Thorne is presently a guest here."

I must be calm. "She was, sir. Minister del Campo and his wife very kindly offered their own home to her. Was that not thoughtful?"

"It was indeed," he agreed. She had just begun to hope that her deflection and name-dropping might have worked when he said, "Sadly, I understand you did not accept his offer. Where is the young lady now?"

"She is out presently. At a playmate's home, I believe."

"You believe? You do not know?" From his tone, she was a

horrible, neglectful parent who did not deserve to have children anywhere near her.

"You know children, Commissario. They might begin at a playmate's home, and before you know it, they are playing kickball in the street, or teaching themselves to steer a gondola, or trying to catch a baby kraken to put in the bath."

"Let us hope not." His face pinched with disgust. "I do not wish to be rude, but I must have the name and address of this playmate."

"Goodness me. Why? Surely the *polizia* can have no interest in an innocent child."

"Ah, but we do. This particular child, it seems, while not under your supervision, was involved in the theft of a valuable object."

Georgia remained as still and relaxed as possible in the face of this bald-faced lie. "How could that be? Cora is not that sort of girl."

"And yet you have known her all of—what? A week, perhaps?"

"Enough to ascertain her character. She has not yet learned to dissemble and deceive."

Unlike some people. Though to give this pleasant man the benefit of the doubt, he could have been fed his information by the Minister and found no reason to disbelieve it.

"The consequences of theft in Venice, Signora, are quite severe. At the time the city was founded, one's hand could be cut off as punishment."

"And today?"

A *thump* sounded from upstairs, which did not at all help her attempts to look relaxed.

"It would depend on the value of the item stolen. In Miss

Thorne's case, a week underwater would likely be her sentence."

She sat upright in alarm, fictional theft or no.

"You have heard, I trust, of the effectiveness of our prison system?"

"I have heard of its barbarity. What a good thing I do not know Cora's immediate whereabouts, if that is to be her fate."

He smiled. "Since the item belonged to the minister's family, it would be up to him to press charges. He might even be persuaded to a lesser charge if she were to return the item. In person, of course."

"What was it, if I might ask?"

"That is confidential, I am afraid."

Of course it was. Impossible to prove—or produce.

"I am unable to help you, sir." She spread her hands and tried to look helpless. "I am merely a tourist, with no knowledge of the names or addresses of people in Venice."

"Unable, or unwilling?"

"Unable, to be sure."

"Then perhaps a walk to the *questura* will help bring the facts to the surface. Please come with me."

"I shall not." Lady Langford stared at him down the length of her nose. "How dare you. The ambassador will hear of this."

"I will deal with His Excellency if and when I must." He stood, and held out a hand. "Come."

"No."

"Do you wish me to arrest you?"

"On what charge, pray?"

"Obstruction of justice, and defiance of an officer in the pursuit of his duty."

"Nonsense. Being unable to provide an address is hardly

an obstruction."

He gazed at her. "In this case, it is. Come. Now."

"No."

"Very well." Before she could move, he had removed a flintlock from a holster on his belt and pointed it at her. With his thumb, he cocked the modified assembly that propelled a bullet at terrifying speeds. "I will not ask you again."

The unblinking eye at the end of the beautifully chased barrel hypnotized her. She rose unsteadily to her feet and as she passed him, he clamped a hand around her upper arm. They proceeded down the stairs, to see Signore Airone standing at the bottom, a bewildered expression on his face and a tea tray in his hands.

"Signora—?"

Verdi snapped a phrase that made the poor man step back in fear.

She did not dare say anything so foolish as "Fetch Signore Seacombe!" for then they would find Cora and her mother. Georgia could do nothing but clamp her lips closed and hope that Millie would contact Sir Ernest before the night was over.

They crossed the receiving hall to the water stairs, where the two officers were already seated in a gondola. She was stuffed rather unceremoniously into the curtained cabin, and held prisoner by hands as immovable as rock. She could not even lunge over the side. Verdi's hand partly covered her nose, so that she couldn't breathe properly. An arm—the one still holding the pistol—was wrapped around her torso.

"If you do not stop wriggling, I will strike you," Verdi said pleasantly in her ear.

Did abusive men practice this silky tone? Hartford had had

it down to an art. White-hot rage flashed through Georgia's body and cleared her head of fear. She was no longer Hart's wife. No man would ever speak to her that way, or treat her that way again. This one would be sorry for it.

She was a model prisoner all the way to their destination, holding her head high when they disembarked at a protected set of water stairs invisible to its neighbors, and disdainfully shaking off the hand that held her. Every moment, she took in her surroundings—pavement, doors, windows, distance to the ground. There were a lot of windows, and stone lacework, and heraldic carvings on this pink villa. Insignia she had seen displayed on a man's chest sash as recently as Tuesday.

She had been conveyed, it seemed, not to the police head-quarters, but to the home of the Minister of Public Works.

This was confirmed as she was shown into a receiving room of faded grandeur, meant to awe and intimidate. Hmph. She had danced in the ballroom at Chatsworth. And even at the much more modest Langford Park, the entrance hall was an example of the best the Georgian period had to offer. Grandeur had no effect upon her.

The minister rose politely as she was escorted in. "Lady Langford. How kind of you to call."

She did not dignify this with a response, simply sat upon the sofa without being invited, so that he was forced to sit as well. Verdi took up a position near the door.

"I am very sorry to have brought you here so peremptorily. I hope you were not inconvenienced?"

"It is quite possible that I will have visible bruises upon my arms and face in the morning," she told him coolly.

He nodded. "I am very sorry, but clearly you were wrong to have resisted."

Oh, so she had brought her bruises upon herself. She had heard that before, too.

"May we get to the point, Minister? I should like this visit to be as brief as possible."

"That will be entirely up to you, Signora. May I assume you have not told the *commissario* of Cora Thorne's whereabouts?"

"If I knew where she was, I would have said so."

"How can you not know where she is? Is she not staying with you?"

"She is with a playmate. I do not know the family's name or address."

"How careless of you. I am astonished."

She merely held his gaze and sent the ball back into his court. "I am curious, Minister, as to why you are so interested in Cora Thorne. She is such an *ordinary* little girl, with no special qualities." *Forgive me, Cora.*

"I am not interested in her in the least," he said without inflection. "But I am deeply interested in her mother's coming to Venice and completing the project she promised me. Has she not been in contact at all?"

Georgia shook her head. "I left word at the late Sir Francis's villa that Cora was in my temporary care, but have had no response as yet, from that quarter or from the embassy. To be truthful, I fear some mishap has waylaid Lady Thorne. For what mother would not come for her child under such circumstances?"

"What mother, indeed. And yet you, by your own admission, have mislaid said child in a most reprehensible manner. I grieve for the state of motherhood in this day and age, I really do."

Georgia made no objection to being painted with the same brush as Louise Thorne. "I do regret being unable to help you," she said. "May I return home?"

"No, you may not. It seems clear that you have withheld information from the fine officers of our *polizia*, and you are now withholding it from me."

"I am not," she said. "I cannot withhold what I do not remember."

"You said you did not know the name and address of this playmate," Commissario Verdi put in. "Not that it had slipped your memory."

"The end result is the same, I am afraid." She lifted one shoulder in a shrug.

"In either case, perhaps a little time to think is in order. Commissario, please take Lady Langford downstairs and ensure she is comfortable."

Georgia did not believe for a moment that this meant a sofa, a good book, and a glass of Chianti.

She was escorted down to the courtyard by her three captors, where she saw that every heavy door was closed and offered no chance of escape. One of the doors led to a set of stone steps winding downward. Verdi lit a lantern and, with an officer's hand planted between her shoulder blades, she was forced to follow him. How could a house have a basement when the entire city was built upon wooden platforms that moved with the gearworks?

When they emerged on a *fondamente*, she heard the lapping of water and the creak and clank of what sounded like metal. Trying to get her bearings, she asked, "Are we still under the villa?"

"Silenzio," Verdi said gruffly. He hung his lantern on an iron hook by the door.

By its wavering light she could see a little way into the dark. The house appeared to have been built on pillars, thick enough to withstand both waves and earthquakes, if their age was any indication. One of them looked distinctly Roman. Over her head hung a chain that was part of a pulley assembly similar to a clothesline. One of the officers reached up to crank a handle, and with a screech, the chain began to move. In a moment, an iron cage large enough to accommodate a slender individual materialized out of the dark, creaking slowly toward them until it scraped the *fondamente*.

"Not that one. I shall take her over," Verdi said.

In spite of herself, cold fear darted through Georgia's stomach. There was nowhere to run. So she straightened her spine and willed herself not to show it.

The assembly took the cage back the way it had come, and presently another appeared, twice its width and a little taller.

It clanked against the *fondamente* until the officer cranked the wheel more quickly and took up the slack in the chain.

"Get in," Verdi said to her, unlatching the barred door and swinging it open.

"Certainly not," she snapped.

Without a word, he took the flintlock out of his pocket and fired it. Something tugged violently on her skirts before the round vanished harmlessly into the water behind her.

Blinking the dazzle of the powder from her eyes, she inspected her walking skirt and gasped. A neat hole with burned edges in the front side panel had a matching hole in the rear. "You beast!"

"Get in, or my aim will be better next time."

Fuming, her heartbeat approaching panic, she stepped into the cage and he got in with her, bringing the lantern with him. She pressed herself against the bars, but still her abused skirts swung around his feet. With a jerk, the cage rounded the horizontal wheel and began its progress out into space.

Georgia swallowed a whimper as they jerked and creaked over a rippling expanse of fathomless black water. The flickering light of the lantern illuminated cages hanging from hooks in the ceiling—cages not attached to the pulley system.

Something lay in the bottom of one. She strained to see —what—?

The light glimmered on bone and she shrieked.

The lantern dipped and swayed as Verdi recovered his grip on it. "What is the matter with you, woman?"

"Sk-keleton!"

He swore in Italian. "That is what happens to people who take too long to answer the Minister's questions."

She had disgraced herself already, so no harm in allowing the whimper building in her throat to turn into a full-on wail. "You will not leave me down here! How long am I—? People will notice I am missing!"

"Perhaps. And we will investigate. Sadly, it will be discovered that you have been the victim of an assassin. Eventually, when they are found, your remains will be returned to England in as ornate a coffin as the Duchy can provide."

"Like Sir Francis?" she said, trying to breathe evenly and failing. "And the gondolier who killed him?"

"The very impressive casket of Sir Francis is already on its way to Munich. Signore Bruno's casket was humble, and appropriate to his station."

They had been right. The *polizia* were in it up to their

necks, taking orders from the minister. What were the odds that the population of assassins in Venice was partly made up of officers of the law?

"Signore Bruno was a father, his youngest only a baby," she said. "You should be ashamed."

The cage clanked against the *fondamente*, throwing her off balance. The chain tightened until they could stand upright, and Verdi pushed open the door. "Out."

She stepped out, leaving him still inside. "What are you—? Wait! You cannot mean to leave me here!"

She stood on a neat square of flagstones about six feet by six, raised a few inches above the water and clearly the top of a plinth. The cage was already moving away, illuminating two similar plinths marching into the darkness. On one lay shadows—bundles of clothing—she shuddered and jerked her frantic gaze away.

"The water is twenty feet deep," Verdi said pleasantly, his voice carrying with chilling clarity across its heaving surface. "And full of krakens. They come and go as they please through this tunnel. You see?"

As it passed, the lantern illuminated the round black maw of a tunnel visible several feet down.

She was already in darkness.

"Enjoy your stay, Lady Langford."

And then there was nothing, only the creak of the chain, the clank of the cage arriving once more at the jetty, a murmur of male voices, and at last, the *thud* of the door.

The lock turned.

Then silence, but for the lapping of the water.

CHAPTER FIFTEEN

*I*t was time to fetch Signore Airone from the family apartments. After reminding an unwilling Lady Thorne that she must stay hidden in the parakeets' room, Millie hurried downstairs and rapped on the door. To her horror, tears lay upon the deeply tanned face that peered out.

"Oh, Signorina," Signore Airone quavered, coming out into the kitchen. "The *polizia* have taken her."

Fear arrowed through Millie's stomach. "When? How long has she been gone?"

"I looked at the clock when I returned the tea tray, and it was eight twenty."

They had missed her by only an hour? Millie groaned. "What did they want?"

"I stayed long enough to hear something about little Cora. The lady sent me for tea, and by the time I prepared it, they were leaving. Signorina—the commissario was holding a flintlock armed with propelled bullets."

Millie's jaw loosened with astonishment. Those were

illegal in England. From within, Lorenzo's voice rose, clearly in agitated conversation with his grandmother, and in a moment, they both joined Millie and Signore Airone in the kitchen.

"Signorina, this is terrible," Lorenzo said, his eyes dark with dismay. "We must tell my grandparents the truth. I cannot have come from conveying you and Lady Langford to the Rialto if she has been here eating dinner and being arrested."

Yes, the time had indeed come to end all secrets among friends.

"The *polizia* and Minister del Campo are determined to get their hands on Cora Thorne and her mother," she said bluntly to the older couple. "The lady who went with me to dinner is Lady Thorne. She is presently upstairs in Cora's room. Lorenzo, would you fetch her here while I explain the situation to your grandparents?"

She did so in rapid, clear Italian, so that by the time Louise Thorne returned with Lorenzo, they were in possession of the facts.

Signore Airone confirmed that the police had taken away the oar and the appointment diary along with a most unwilling Georgia. The diary, at least, seemed to indicate who might be behind this extreme exercise of the law.

"I believe that when Lady Langford would not tell them where Cora is, they arrested her and have in all likelihood taken her to the Minister." Millie then translated what she had said for Louise. "The question now is, what can we do to help her other than send an urgent message to the ambassador? For he must intervene without delay."

"It is vital that Lady Thorne's whereabouts remain secret." Lorenzo's grandfather gazed at his new guest and spoke in his halting English. "You will be forced to give the minister what he wants, Signora, and will be a prisoner thereafter. He will disavow all knowledge of you to the outside world. It has happened before," he concluded darkly.

Signora Airone murmured something to her husband in the Veneziano dialect that Millie could not quite catch.

He nodded and turned back to them. "My wife believes that Lady Thorne and her child must leave Venice by the fastest means. If they remain in the city, the minister will not cease his questioning and even torture of Lady Langford until he has them in hand."

"Dear heaven," Millie managed, her knees going weak. "Torture?"

"Once they are safe, we can let it be known that they have left the city or met with a fatal accident. We must hope that Lady Langford has a strong constitution until the truth frees her."

He clamped his lips shut upon further details. If he thought to spare Millie's feelings, he had achieved exactly the opposite. But she must not dwell on that or she would collapse in a fit of hysterics.

"We had thought to go out to Signore van Meere's airship, and hide aboard it," Louise said. "But we lack a means of concealment for the journey—to say nothing of a boat."

"I do not know this person," Signore Airone said. "If this ship is moored on the Lido, it will not be permitted to leave without a search if you are known to be at large."

"It isn't moored there," Louise told him. "It's enormous.

There wasn't room on the Lido for it, so he has it moored on an island somewhere."

"I know where it is," Lorenzo said. "On the far side of Murano, on an islet inhabited only by gulls and pelicans. The vaporetto captains are laughing over it, for only a boat with a shallow draft can reach it, and the man had a lot of luggage and crew. If he is trying to be discreet, he is failing. The fuselage is the size of a thundercloud, looming over the lagoon."

"If they are already making a joke of it, perhaps no one will think to look there," Signore Airone said.

Once more his wife murmured in his ear, and this time his brows rose. He reached around her and gave her a squeeze, and a smacking kiss. When he turned back, the signora was beet red and Lorenzo grinning from ear to ear.

"My grandmother is brilliant," the young man said. "Her brother is a fisherman, selling his catch each morning at the Rialto market. She will ask him to take you over to the island in his boat, concealed under canvas."

Goodness. So simple, and yet so very dangerous.

"I cannot ask your grand-uncle to endanger himself for me," Louise said. "There must be another way."

"Every way will be under surveillance by morning, Signora," Lorenzo said. He spoke quickly to his grandmother, who nodded and went back into a bedroom. She returned in a moment wrapping a shawl over her head and shoulders. With a dip of her head, she departed through the kitchen door.

"My wife has gone to inform her brother he will have passengers," Signore Airone said. "Can Signora Thorne and the child be ready to leave here at three of the clock?"

"We can," Louise said without hesitation. "If Lorenzo will

convey Cora here, he can take us out to the fishing boat. But what about Georgia?"

"Once you are away," Millie said, "I will go to the embassy and demand that Sir Ernest act immediately. When Georgia is secured, you may be certain we will depart Venice by the fastest possible means."

"Then … I will not see you again after tonight?" Louise took Millie's cold hands in hers. "It is a very abrupt end to a friendship, I must say."

"I hope it is not the end," Millie told her, a lump forming in her throat in spite of her determination to be brave. "I hope all this is just … an interruption."

"I hope so, too." Louise squeezed her fingers. "I must collect my few bits from the roof, which the police did not search. We have come to a pretty pass when Cora's luggage is quite three times the size of mine."

Millie kissed her. "I will go with Lorenzo to fetch her. I must tell Mr Seacombe what has happened. And with any luck, neither the police nor an assassin will barge in here within the next five hours to undo all our good work."

Twenty minutes later, Millie found herself once more in front of the heavy door that faced the street where the Seacombes were staying. She turned the knob, but it was, of course, locked. Did one simply knock at this time of night and expect to be heard?

She rapped on the door, and when she could hear no one approaching, pounded on it with one fist.

Leisurely footsteps sounded in the street behind her, and she whirled. A dark silhouette moved into the flickering light of a lamp set in an embrasure and removed a shape that could only be a Stetson.

"Mr Seacombe!" she gasped. "Goodness, you gave me a fright."

He peered at her. "Miss Brunel? Has something happened?"

"Yes," she said with admirable brevity. "May we go in? Time is of the essence."

He unlocked the door and ushered her into the courtyard. She followed him up the steps to his flat, where Marcus, in a nightshirt, sat at the table with a mug of milky tea, Cora opposite him enjoying another.

"Why aren't you two rascals in bed?" Mr Seacombe inquired. "I could swear I saw you go up."

"I couldn't sleep," Cora said. "I was wishing I could run away to the Villa dei Pappagalli to be with Mama."

"Then Lorenzo and I are here to make your wish come true," Millie said. "Lady Langford has been taken away by the police. They want to know where you are. Therefore, we must get you and your mama out to Mr van Meere's airship tonight."

Without a word, Mr Seacombe rose and went into another room. When he returned, he was strapping on a leather belt from which hung two six-guns in holsters.

Marcus's eyes widened. "Dad! You ain't going to the *questura*, are you?"

"No, he is not," Millie said firmly, before he could reply. "There is no need for firearms, sir. What we need is secrecy and speed. Cora, you are to come with me. Some four hours from now, at three o'clock, Signora Airone's brother the fisherman will hide you and your mother on his fishing boat and take you out to *Foresight*."

"That means I'm going, too!" Marcus said in delight. "So I

can let you in."

"That is up to your father, young man."

"Have to say I wouldn't mind," Mr Seacombe said. "Guess I'd better notify the crew, too. I have a feeling our sojourn here is coming to a rapid end."

"May I just say that I don't approve of doing this without Mr van Meere's permission?" Millie's protests would do no good, but once again, she must make them.

"If I need to tell him, I will. But until then, no. Marcus, take your rucksack. May as well be thorough. We don't know how much longer Mr van Meere will be in Venice, but best not to have to come back here. You'll stay with the ladies and provide what services they require of you."

"Yes sir!" Clearly elated, Marcus ran from the room.

"And you, Miss Brunel?" Mr Seacombe said. "You're the last man standing, it seems."

Did he have to phrase it quite that way? "I shall be on the ambassador's doorstep at first light, demanding his assistance to have Georgia released. I shall not take no for an answer."

"I'd buy a ticket to see that." He smiled, his eyes warm. "And if diplomatic channels fail?"

"Then—then—" Her gaze fell on the holstered six-guns. "Then it will be your turn."

"Fair enough."

She met his eyes once more. "Where were you coming from, just now? When I met you outside?"

"Would you believe me if I said a saloon?"

"No, much as I would like to."

"I was visiting *i monaci*. My friend there believes matters are coming to a head with regard to the murder of Sir Francis. They weren't happy to hear their report to the *questura* was buried and the victim's family lied to. He was distressed to have confirmation of the rumor that the Minister means to have his breakwater even if people die for it."

"Why is it so important to del Campo?" Millie asked. "It is not as if *he* is going to wear the crown." He did not reply. After a moment, she added, "Is he?"

"Del Campo is all too happy to tell you he has de Medici blood."

He had mentioned it, in fact, while they were dancing. And she had thought he was merely making a joke, believing she was an Englishwoman whose idea of history was cloudy.

"The Doge is elected, as you might know," Mr Seacombe went on. "Some folks think the dukedom ought to come to a man by right of blood, not by a vote."

"I see." And once the man had the duchy behind his breakwater, he could not only defy his king and queen, but quietly do away with the Doge, too, and declare himself king.

The children ran back in, dressed and carrying all their worldly goods in the form of Cora's traveling closet and valise, and Marcus's bulging rucksack. "Bye, Dad." The boy threw his arms around his father.

"Keep your eyes open and your boots on, son." Mr Seacombe gave him a bear hug.

And then it was all Millie could do to keep up with their two small shadows, the trunk bumping along behind, until they reached the public jetty on the canal where Lorenzo waited.

May 11, 1895, at 2:20 a.m.

Of all the terrifying aspects of her situation, Georgia

considered the worst to be Commissario Verdi's taking the lamp with him.

Whether her eyes were closed or open, it made no difference in the Stygian darkness of the dungeon under the house's foundations. Her sense of hearing, though, seemed to have become more acute. Along with the lapping of the waves against the stone plinth, the *plink* of droplets falling from some height, the rush of a wake, came the inevitable speculation about what was causing all those sounds.

Had a kraken surfaced? Were its tentacles even now reaching for her?

Shivering, she did not dare take a step in any direction lest she plummet into the water. So she sat, cross legged, after having turned her bullet-holed skirt up over her head to form a shawl for warmth.

She must do something. She must think.

For it had been borne in upon her that in treating a baron's widow in this way, Minister del Campo had shown his hand. He had no intention of setting her free to regale the nearest representative of Her Majesty with her tale of woe. Verdi had been perfectly serious about the coffin that would be donated by the city to befit said widow's station.

Therefore, she must pre-empt her own death at their hands. She must escape. The difficulty lay in the certainty of death at her own hands should she try.

Into her memory came Millie's voice, soft with the discovery of new knowledge. *They are imprisoned, not by the krakens, but by their own fear.*

How very apropos. And how quick Verdi had been to mock her by pointing out that underwater tunnel to freedom. He had known perfectly well that no one imprisoned down here would escape, though the way was clear. Only *in extremis* would a person fling themselves to the krakens, counting it better to die quickly than to linger any longer in the wreck of their hopes ... or starvation.

But what had Louise Thorne been saying that Millie had replied to? *There is nothing to dread in the krakens.* And something about a monograph discussing electrical fields and thought transference. Georgia wished now she had paid greater attention, asked more questions, but at the time it had sounded like something the Educated Gentleman might have published in his *Tales of a Medicine Man.* Well, if she ever got out of here, she would write to the newspaper that carried his stories and enclose a full account, in case he ever needed inspiration.

"You are not going to escape by that means, my girl, no matter what Louise thinks," she said aloud. Her voice seemed to whisper off stone walls and pillars. "Trusting your life to a stranger's thesis? Are you mad?"

Something brushed her knee and she nearly leaped out of her skin.

Crablike, she scuttled back, but then her hand fell on the lip of the stone platform and she stopped, panting, willing the panic to subside. She must not sit near the edge. She must get as close to the middle as she could, where it could not reach her.

But how long were a kraken's tentacles?

Whimpering, she could only estimate where the middle of the plinth was, and draw herself into as small a bundle as possible, wrapping the hems of her turned-up skirt tightly around her.

All right, then. All four sides were impossible. Below was unthinkable.

She must look above. A chain had conveyed the cages to the landing, had it not? The cage had been only a little taller than Verdi, and hung down about a foot on its connecting hook. If she were to jump, she ought to be able to reach the chain.

And then what? Traverse hand over hand—without losing her grip and falling in—to the wheel that turned the whole enterprise?

He locked the door, you ninny. You cannot go that way.

Something touched her knee again, and she screamed.

"Get away!" Hands flailing, she slapped at whatever it was, but it was too quick for her.

A tendril, cool and wet, wound around her wrist.

Had anyone ever gone mad with panic? Died of it?

She could never remember what happened in the next dreadful seconds. But the shock of her sudden plunge into the cold water brought her to her senses.

She fought her way to the surface, the tentacle still wrapped around her wrist, and gasped for air. One thrashing hand landed on the edge of the platform on which she'd been sitting, but getting up there was out of the question. The creature would just pull her back in.

Or … well, what the devil was it waiting for?

Her skirts floated up around her chest as the tentacle unwound from her wrist and tapped her clenched fist, as though it wanted her to open her fingers.

Had she hit her head? Was she unconscious? Was this a dream?

Bemused, she opened her hand, palm up. In the water,

blue-white particles moved with the current, sparkling like tiny stars. The tentacle applied its suckers to her skin with infinite gentleness, like nothing so much as a gentleman's kiss.

Was it ... *tasting* her?

Oh, heaven help me. Make my death quick. Teddy, oh Teddy, my darling boy—

A picture filled her head. In it, she saw herself, white-faced and wide-eyed, held by the tentacle, which was attached— after several coils—to a kraken with large, soft eyes. In the vision, another tentacle touched her face. She felt it, as light as a mother's caress of a sleeping child.

Definitely a dream. All right, then. She would behave as one did in dreams, and simply go along with it.

I am called Georgia. Are you a friend?

In the vision, the beast tapped her hand. She felt it, no longer tasting or smelling, but replying in the affirmative.

I am glad.

The tentacles wriggled, and it gave a slow blink, as though she had pleased it.

May we leave this place through the tunnel?

The vision melted, and she seemed to be looking into a recollection. A speedy journey through the tunnel, passing other krakens on the way, and then a swift ascent, where sunlight wavered underwater much the way it did on the surface.

May we go together? To the surface?

She barely had time to fill her lungs before she was enfolded in the kraken's embrace and pulled under. She was utterly blinded, yet she could see their progress along the tunnel through the beast's consciousness, its many tentacles moving with such concerted strength that she could feel her skirts beating around her ankles with the speed of their going.

And then they were through, and out in the open lagoon. Through the eyes and memory of her escort, she saw its depth, the vast bronze arcs of the gearworks disappearing into the darkness, little cars like bubbles with men inside, ascending and descending upon the massive cogs.

Prisoners. Cleaning the gearworks.

But to the kraken, they were merely a curiosity and sometimes food. It swam upward, and at length she could see with her own eyes—or at least, with her own sight combined with the beast's memory of the surface like a greenish-blue miracle. For, she remembered with a sense of shock, it was still night.

Her head broke the surface and she dragged air into her lungs—sweet, cool air smelling of seaweed, God be praised—half gasping, half weeping.

Thank you thank you.

The kraken did not surface, though it held her as though it knew she needed a moment to recover from its headlong swim. Instead, another picture filled her mind, of the vast lagoon. She appeared to be about halfway between Saluté and the Lido, if the twinkling lights on either hand were any indication.

A tentacle broke the surface next to her ear, its end curling up and then out. It looked for all the world as though it were asking, *What now?*

A very good question indeed. She had discarded the fancy of a dream several minutes ago, and now must return to the practicalities of having succeeded in breaking out of gaol. The Lido was closer, but—

The Lido. The airfield. And a Zeppelin-built airship named after Thetis, goddess of the sea.

May we go to that island, there? Where men's airships are moored?

A picture formed in her mind of the Lido by night, with the fuselages ranged in neat ranks in the grass, puzzling and strange to a sea creature.

Yes. That one.

Once again she was enfolded in its tentacles, she filled her lungs, and they ducked beneath the waves. The beast swam so fast that her hair, long ago having lost its pins, billowed out behind her. She had to close her eyes against the force of the water. But the kraken's picture in her head was as good as vision, showing the underwater slopes of the island coming into view and then flattening as they drew nearer to shore.

Her head broke the surface once again, and in the next moment, her feet found purchase in the sand.

Gasping for breath, up to her chin in seawater, Georgia turned to face the creature who floated on the bottom, concealing itself from anyone's sight but her own. It was so large that its carapace was clearly visible, its tentacles curling around her as though it feared she might lose her footing.

You have saved my life. I am so grateful. I will be all right from here.

A picture formed in her head of a blond girl with a beautiful smile whom she had never seen before, floating in the water in much the same way. An air of affection suffused the picture. Then the vision changed, as the beast turned a little so that one eye could take her in, and she saw herself once again as it saw her.

She put all the affection and gratitude she possessed into

her own smile, and touched the end of one tentacle with the palm of her hand, so that its suckers clung to it.

With a slow blink of satisfaction, the animal drifted away into deeper water, trailing its glimmering sparks of light.

Thank you, friend.

And with a wriggle of its tentacles like a wave, it was gone.

CHAPTER SIXTEEN

MAY 11, 1895 AT 3:10 A.M.

$\mathcal{M}$arcus was too excited to sleep, though his head and Cora's were pillowed on his rucksack in the bottom of the gondola. He heard Lady Thorne's impatient exhalations as she attempted to find a comfortable way to lie under the canvas that covered them. Lorenzo was taking no chances. A single gondolier might plausibly return from a late-night fare at three in the morning, but a vessel bearing a woman and children would certainly draw attention, even if it were the benign sort. Marcus knew from experience that attention meant memories, and memories could mean discovery.

It seemed to take ages, listening to the water gurgle under the gondola's hull and smelling mildew in the old canvas Lorenzo had unearthed from somewhere. But at length, a low voice hailed them and the gunwale of the gondola bumped up against something hard. A moment later, the canvas was whisked away and Marcus sat up.

Lady Thorne woke Cora softly, and the two of them slid

carefully up on to the seat, so as not to upset the gondola's trim.

A rope ladder unrolled itself into the boat right on top of Marcus. After he fought his way free of it, Lorenzo nodded to him. "You first. Help the ladies at the top."

Rucksack on his back, he made short work of the ladder. From the gunwale of the fishing boat, he could see the night lights of the city. They were at the mouth of the Grand Canal, too far from either bank for anyone to see them clearly, but they were still boarding on the seaward side, just in case anyone was lounging about with a spyglass.

Lady Thorne sent Cora up first. She climbed fast, considering this was probably the first time she'd gone up a rope ladder on deep water. She went over the gunwale on her stomach, and Marcus was obliged to pull her in and set her right way up before she caught a facer on the deck. Her traveling closet went up after her.

Lady Thorne, rider of steamcycles and designer of things people would kill for, was clearly a woman of skills. She tossed her skirts over one shoulder and climbed every bit as neatly as Marcus had himself, and when he offered her his hand on the last bit, she took it with a smile though she did not need it at all.

Marcus did not complain at holding her hand. It felt nice, and she squeezed it before she let go of it.

"Down on the deck, if you please, behind these nets," the older man—Lorenzo's grand-uncle—said in a low voice. Marcus and the ladies obeyed, though he could tell that Lady Thorne was making a heroic effort to do so. Lorenzo said farewell, though they could not answer. Sound carried over water.

In a moment, a rumbling came from below decks as the steam engine was ignited. Marcus would have liked to see it, but this was no time for curiosity. Another eternity passed as they came about and plowed through the water of the lagoon, the waves smacking the hull and gurgling around the keel. The engine was cut, and with a grinding sound, the anchor ran out.

"You can stand up now," the man said in the Veneziano dialect, which Marcus had just enough of to understand about one word in three.

"He says it's safe to come out," he told Cora and her mother.

They rose from their hiding place and found themselves under the swelling bulk of *Foresight*'s massive fuselage. A heron croaked in irritation at being disturbed before dawn, and Marcus heard several cormorants dive into the water in alarm. The birds were the sole inhabitants of this island, which was probably about the size of the fuselage. The airship tugged at its mooring irons as the dawn breeze passed over the water, and its ropes creaked.

"How do we get over there?" Cora asked.

He looked at their pilot, who jerked his chin toward the islet. "Swim."

Marcus translated.

"Bollocks," said Lady Thorne, her shoulders going slack with yet another task to accomplish.

"Mama!" Cora remonstrated, clearly shocked.

"Well, there's nothing for it. We can peg our clothes out to dry when the sun comes up. On the bright side, I shall be able to go without a corset all day."

"Mama!"

188

This time, Marcus took off his boots and went over first, partly so he could assist from below, and partly to get away from any further mention of … unmentionables. The draft of the fishing boat must be awfully shallow, for he was able to touch the bottom right away. He held his rucksack and boots up out of reach of the waves, placed them on the dry sand, then went back for Cora's trunk. She removed her own boots and jumped in to help him, Lady Thorne bringing up the rear.

The three of them waded to shore, and turned to wave their thanks to Lorenzo's grand-uncle, who waved back and then set his course eastward to the fishing grounds.

"That's that accomplished," Lady Thorne said, her own boots hanging around her neck as she wrung out her skirts on the narrow beach. Her blouse was still dry, but he didn't know whereabouts a corset ended, so it might be soaked, too. "Marcus, stage two is up to you. Cora and I will meet you at the gangway."

"Can you take my rucksack?"

She pulled it off his shoulders, and promptly dropped it with a clank, as though she hadn't expected it to weigh so much. "What have you got in here? Spare parts?"

"Some," he said. "It never hurts to have a few, does it?"

"Spoken like a true engineer—I quite agree. I hope you've room left for a spare shirt, at least. Come along, Cora, and let Marcus do his job."

"I want to go with him, Mama. I might need to know someday how to board an airship secretly."

Lady Thorne hesitated, then thought better of what she'd been going to say. "Off you go, then. I'll take your things around to the gangway."

Foresight was built like a battleship, with the engineering gondola aft and the captain and navigation crew in a larger one forward. In pods below both gondolas were the guns, accessible from above through a hatch. Marcus gave Cora the running tour as they made their way to the stern.

"But where are the crew?" she asked. "Surely they aren't aboard."

"They're in the town until Dad sends word that Mr van Meere might be ready to lift. They're billeted near the Arsenale, with the pilots of other ships." He looked up. "Here we are."

Pigeons came and went to airships through a chute that led into the communications cage, where they shelved themselves until their contents could be examined and they were sent on their next mission. "It's easy to get out—you just slide down it," he told Cora. "A bit trickier getting in."

"If you can do it, I can," she said. "A spy has to know that trick."

He couldn't argue. Those boys in his street could learn a thing or two about pluck from Cora Thorne.

"*Foresight* and the ships of the Albion Line are probably the easiest to board this way," he said. "The chute is big enough to allow somebody our size to get in. It's the little ones that you have to get into the hard way—shimmy up the mooring ropes, scale the fuselage on the nets, and go in through the dorsal hatch."

She made a face. "I'll stop thinking what I was thinking about Mr van Meere needing such a big ship, then."

He bounced a couple of times, jumped, and swung himself into the mouth of the chute. Sand clittered as it rubbed off his damp bare feet.

"Go up like a spider, using your hands and feet pressing against the sides."

The brass was cold, since dawn was a long way off yet. But his warm hands and feet stuck to it just fine, and in a moment he was in the cage, turning to give Cora a hand so she could scramble up beside him.

"See? Easy as a wink."

"I won't be able to do this when I'm grown up," she said sadly as they got to their feet. "While we're waiting out here, though, I could practice the external entry, on the mooring ropes and nets."

They ran forward through the dim, silent ship. It smelled of baking and cigars and furniture polish and dust. Dad would say it needed a good many of the viewing ports opened. At the gangway, he shoved the lever down and it lowered obediently, coming to rest on the tussocky grass about a foot from Lady Thorne's boots.

"Nicely done," she said with a smile, strolling up the incline to them. "I hadn't even got to one hundred. Do you suppose there's anything to eat aboard this behemoth? I don't know about you, but once I have had an hour or two of sleep, I shall be ready for breakfast."

4:20 a.m.

The full moon lay far to the west, which meant Georgia didn't have a lot of time before the sky began to lighten with dawn. She had been taken to the minister's palace at about nine, and spent less than an hour in his odious company before being marched down to the dungeon. After that, she had no idea how long she had been alone and shivering and even dozing a little in exhaustion before the kraken arrived to investigate. In any case, the little chronometer pinned to her blouse had stopped working after its sudden plunge into the water.

She wrung out her skirts and mourned the sad ruin of her favorite suede half-boots. They would need to serve her a little longer, however, for she wasn't about to take them off and roam about the airfield barefoot.

The Lido was not fenced. Apparently the Venetians considered the lagoon protection enough from thievery ... unless there was also a night watchman for that purpose. She would have to be careful. The difficulty was that she had no idea where *Thetis* was moored. There appeared to be no option but to run from one vessel to the next, straining to read names by moonlight and the light of the occasional lantern on a pole.

My kingdom for a moonglobe.

Then again, a moonglobe bobbing along between ships was certain to attract attention. She would have to do the best she could. Twenty or so ships of the right size. That couldn't take more than twenty minutes, could it?

Ducking under gondolas and fuselages, dodging mooring ropes, she moved as quickly as she was able down the row. The guard tower standing in the middle of the field was rather a shock, for it hadn't been visible from the beach. She thanked her lucky stars she had not been running down the broad, grassy aisle between ranks of ships before she'd seen it, for inside were two watchmen on the lower level, and four more men on the guns at the top.

Wait—*guns?*

Panting, she paused in the black shadow of a vessel's fuselage to gape at the watch tower. Why had she not noticed when *Juno* had landed that there was an armed tower here? Why had it never come up in conversations with Mr Seacombe? Oh, she was certainly going to have words with him if she ever saw him again—for heaven's sake, those barrels were big enough to be cannon!

It was going to be difficult enough to get the engines ignited and *Thetis* cast off without benefit of navigator, engineer, or ground crew. And now to find out she could be shot out of the sky in the attempt? Oh, after all she'd been through tonight, it was just too much!

She came *this close* to collapsing in the grass to have a good cry.

Buck up, Georgia. She might not be able to leave just now, but the same staff couldn't man the tower twenty-four hours a day. They would have to change at some point, and she might have her chance then.

She made sure to keep the bulk of the next two ships between herself and the tower. At the next one, three from the easternmost end of the field, she slipped under the fuselage to look up at the gondola's bow. It took a moment for the name to register. *Thetis.*

"Found you," she whispered.

Now to get in. The ship had been close-hauled to the ground and a sign pounded into the grass where the gangway would normally rest. She couldn't read much of it, but the arms of the Duchy and official-looking print gave her to understand that the vessel was the temporary property of the Doge.

Hmph. A fig for your impound. I'm stealing this ship and the Doge can go to the devil.

She had never regretted incurring her mother-in-law's eternal disdain by learning to pilot an airship early in her marriage. Like cooking, one was supposed to have people to do that sort of thing, not do it oneself. Even then, not yet twenty-two, Georgia had understood that knowing how to fly might save her life someday. The same principle had applied during her recovery from Teddy's birth, when behind Hart's back, she had demanded of the coachman that he teach her how to pilot a steam landau, right down to filling its boiler with water and knowing where to oil the acceleration bar assembly.

She might not be an engineer, but at least she had made herself able to run away under her own steam. And now she was running away with a vengeance. She would fly to Geneva, march straight to the authorities, and secure assistance to rescue Millie, Louise, and Cora. But first, she must get into *Thetis's* sleek gondola.

Did this model allow the gangway to be lowered from outside? Many did—Hart's included. But she could not see a lever. At the rear of the gondola, there was only the chute for the communications cage, and nothing larger than a pigeon—brass or feathered—was going in that way.

"Bother it." She was going to have to scale the fuselage and go in through the dorsal hatch, like an aeronaut. Why couldn't Sir Francis have owned an airship with an automaton intelligence system? They were all the rage in England, Teddy said, now that—

She looked up at the numbers on the fuselage and recollected that this was a Zeppelin-built vessel. The intelligence system came standard in the newer ones. Which she only knew because Teddy had been wild to replace Hart's out-of-date tub before he went up to Oxford, and had been leaving Lady Claire Malvern's and Lady Alice Hollys's treatises describing their invention of the system in places where he knew she couldn't miss them.

Georgia marched over to the gangway and said clearly, in as close an approximation of Louise's alto voice and Kentish accent as she could, "*Thetis*, lower gangway."

For a moment, nothing happened. Then a seam appeared in the hull, and the gangway lowered to the grass so quickly she had to jump out of its way. In a trice, she was galloping up the ramp and pushing up the lever at the top to close it again.

"Well done, *Thetis*," she gasped.

She ran into the navigation gondola and peered out of the nearest viewing port. Nothing moved in the sleeping airfield, and there were still six men on the watch tower.

But something was moving on the beach. A boat was nosing in, and half a dozen men were in the process of leaping out to drag it up on the sand. She had gained sanctuary just in time.

Then she realized what it might mean, and her heart sank. Were they massing to launch some kind of attack on *Thetis*?

But no, black figures were marching down the stairs inside the struts of the tower. Shift change.

Now was her chance!

"*Thetis*, ignite boiler but not engines. Prepare to lift."

Nothing happened.

Bother it! Of course the ground crew had shut down the boiler. Del Campo expected to put the ship to auction, probably, after he murdered the entire Thorne family.

Georgia ran aft down the corridor to the engine room. Several levers lay in the down position. She rammed them upward and the interior systems came awake. "*Thetis*, ignite boiler." The familiar sounds were like music to her ears. "Good girl. Come to full pressure, but do not ignite engines until I say so."

It was still dark outside. What were the odds that she could cast off ropes and lift? Could *Thetis* rise out of range of the guns before anyone noticed? Airborne, she could then ignite the engines and make way.

She must try. There was some comfort in knowing that even if they did shoot her down, she had some chance of surviving the fall and ending up in the lagoon. The thought of the krakens backing her up was a comfort.

Now for the mooring ropes.

Opening the gangway again meant a risk, since it was in full view of the beach, but she had to take it. Four ropes. The knots were thick and unfamiliar, but she untied them by feel, keeping low and in the shadows as much as she could.

Three ropes. She could hear the men talking to one another down the beach. At least it masked the whisper of the boiler coming up to flight pressure.

Two ropes. She had left the one closest to the gangway for last. With hasty fingers, she worked the knot. Whoever had winched the ship down nearly to ground level had a heavy hand with a knot.

At last she got it undone and tossed it aside. Halfway up the gangway, she heard a shout.

She couldn't understand the Italian, but she understood the tone all too well.

The jig was up.

She had just enough time to raise the gangway before she felt the deck press up under her feet. Her knees bent with the swift rise of the vessel. *Please, please, please,* she prayed incoherently. A spray of bullets was one thing, but nothing could withstand the guns on the tower.

Something pinged off the hull practically under her feet and she leaped aside by instinct. Someone had fired a rifle from the beach. The guns wouldn't be far behind.

She was out of time. Running to the gondola, she shouted, "*Thetis*, ignite engines. Set course north, top speed."

Two things happened at once.

The lovely Daimler engines rumbled smoothly into life at full pressure, and Georgia staggered as *Thetis* put her shoulder into the turn.

And with a flash of angry light, two cannons boomed a fusillade of death from the top of the watch tower.

CHAPTER SEVENTEEN

5:05 A.M.

*W*ith Mr Seacombe and his six-guns at her side like a grim shadow, Millie pounded on the door of the embassy with a fist. A minute passed, and in the light of the lamp over the door, she could see her companion eyeing the lock, one thumb stroking the grip of the pistol.

To her relief, he decided against shooting it off and pounded on the door himself.

A moment later, the door opened to reveal the majordomo she had seen before, managing the luncheon so efficiently after Sir Francis's funeral.

"We must see Sir Ernest immediately," she said in Italian, with all the authority she could command. "It is a matter of life and death."

To his credit, the man did not sputter or argue, simply showed them upstairs to the ambassador's private apartments, into a library that Millie had not seen before. Then he vanished. Perhaps he had had more than his share of people in similar situations.

After a dreadful quarter of an hour in which Millie could

not even find comfort in the spines of the books, or converse in more than disjointed phrases with Mr Seacombe, Sir Ernest came in, fully dressed. She would consider trousers, shirt, and waistcoat fully dressed, at least, given the hour.

"My dear lady, whatever is the matter?" he asked. "My man has said it is a matter of life and death."

As succinctly as she could, Millie told him everything, right down to the minister's invitation upon the balcony of this very embassy, and how it tied into the death of Sir Francis.

Sir Ernest sat rather heavily in a brocade reading chair. "Go on."

"Of course we have no proof that Sir Francis's death was not at the hands of an anonymous assassin. The proof we did have was seized by Commissario Verdi of the *polizia*, very likely on the minister's orders."

"What proof is this?"

"A cracked oar with a hair from Sir Francis's head caught in it, for one. And the second you brought to us yourself—his appointment diary, showing far too many meetings with Minister del Campo and various others involved in the break-water project than could be explained by diplomacy. They were hoping to use him, you see, to get Lady Thorne here against her will. That is why he was instructed to bring Cora with him. Her mother did not know he had effectively kidnapped her until they reached Venice."

"We must cable her at once, then, and tell her not to come."

"She is already here," Mr Seacombe said. "In a safe location."

"There are no safe locations in the Duchy," the ambassador said with more truth than diplomacy.

"It was the best we could do." Mr Seacombe said no more.

"And how does Lady Langford figure into this? Is she also in a safe location?"

"Indeed not." Millie leaned forward. "She was seized at the same time as the evidence, and taken away for questioning."

"Her crime, Miss Brunel?" He did not add *this time*.

"She would not, we believe, reveal Cora's location so that she could be used as bait to capture Lady Thorne."

"I see," Sir Ernest said thoughtfully. "So you are telling me that what remains of the Thorne family is in danger because Minister del Campo wants Lady Thorne to work on the breakwater? But she has already been commissioned to do so. I don't understand."

"She found out it is to be armed," Millie said, doing her best to speak clearly above her pounding heart. "It is our belief that the Doge wishes to wall off the city, isolate the port, and use that pressure to force the king and queen to allow the Duchy to become an independent kingdom. Then he would declare himself king."

Sir Ernest stared. "Preposterous. And impossible, after unification. What do you mean, your belief? Have you any proof of all this?"

"Only the word of Lady Thorne."

"And is she in the confidence of the minister?" His eyebrows were climbing as well as his incredulous tone.

"She was, I think, before she found out that the breakwater was to surround the city like a moat and be armed with cannon. At which point she refused to work on the project any longer."

"Armed with cannon?" he exclaimed. "Are you mad, madam?"

"Easy there," said Mr Seacombe. "It's a lot to take in, we know. But there's no need to throw insults."

"Following her refusal," Millie went on, determined to tell all despite this reception of her information, "the minister began his campaign of coercion, since nothing else would work. She is a lady of spirit and resolution, is Lady Thorne. But he has no compunction about using children for his own ends."

The ambassador appeared to control his next words with an effort of will. "What do you want me to do, Miss Brunel? Order the minister to stop his nonsense, and sit down for a cup of tea?"

A flush burned into Millie's cheeks. She had trusted this man, but now he sounded just like her nephew Hartford when he was cornered, his only weapon sarcasm and the use of belittlement to cut an opponent—or a problem—down to a manageable size.

She must reiterate, it was clear, the most immediate problem.

"We need your help to have Lady Langford released. The rest is no business of ours, though it may be England's. But the arrest of a baron's widow, who has committed no crime, must not be allowed to stand."

"I have already come to her aid once. Can she not be trusted to stay out of gaol?"

Mr Seacombe shifted in his chair. And while Millie fought with her own temper and the scalding words that wanted to spill out on the ambassador's head, he forestalled her.

"You do not believe us, that's plain," he said in his gravelly voice. "But an innocent lady has been taken out of her home in the night and as of twenty minutes ago, has not been returned. At the very least you must demand that she be released into your custody. If they refuse, you might have a clue that we're not just spinning a tall tale."

"If they refuse, it will be because they have proof of their charges," Sir Ernest said. "What are they, by the way?"

"We do not know. She was taken when I was out at dinner," Millie said.

"At dinner where?"

"As it happens, at my lodgings," Mr Seacombe said.

The ambassador looked disappointed. "I cannot very well risk my relationship with the Duchy's government by asking the police to look the other way on Lady Langford's behalf a second time. But I will send someone to find out the charges. Then we may bring one of our barristers to bear upon the case."

"But that could take days," Millie exclaimed. "Lady Langford must be freed this morning!"

"Does she have pressing engagements?" he inquired.

Millie lost her temper. "Of course not," she snapped. "She is in gaol because she would not assist in the coercion of an internationally known engineer. Any charges they trump up to justify it will be lies, and you know it."

"I know nothing." He rose to his feet with dignity. "And in the absence of proof, nor do you. Your loyalty to your companion does you credit, but there are larger forces at work here. I will deal with this through diplomatic channels."

Run along, little lady, and let the men run the world.

Millie could not breathe properly. Her lungs had constricted with rage and fear. Blindly, she rose and found Mr Seacombe's arm ready to assist her. As they were shown out, she realized she was gripping him so tightly that her fingers had formed claws, digging into the sleeve of his long, swinging coat.

"I am so sorry," she gasped as they gained the square and began the twenty-minute walk back to the Villa dei Pappagalli.

"Think nothing of it."

The sky arched over them, the clear aqua color of the sea, and the Grand Canal glowed gold and pink with the imminence of dawn. Shopkeepers and the inhabitants of the villas were busy washing the streets, sweeping the water into the canals. Another day had begun, a city unaware that a woman was missing. That a mother and child had been forced into hiding. That a gondolier had been murdered. That a diplomat had not in fact fallen out of his evening's transportation.

So many industrious people, unaware that another world entirely was operating under the familiar one they knew.

"What are we going to do?" she whispered. "I cannot bear to wait until he locates a barrister."

"If he even plans to."

"That's just it."

Millie looked up into Mr Seacombe's grim face, where a muscle was working in his jaw. He was grinding his teeth.

"I wonder what brought about this change of heart?" she said. "Sir Ernest has been solicitude itself until now. He has done everything possible to help us. And now we must accept *diplomatic channels?*"

"He said it himself. There are larger forces at work here. Someone has been leaning on him, and I can guess whom."

Millie paced silently beside him for the length of a lane, before they crossed a bridge and came into their own neighborhood. In the distance she could see the roof of the Villa dei Pappagalli.

"We are on our own, aren't we?" she said at last.

"I'd say so, yep."

"What are we going to do?" Her lips trembled with fear for Georgia, and she could not even find the spine to be ashamed when he looked down just in time to see a tear roll down her cheek.

He stopped on the *fondamente* and enfolded her in a hug such as he might have given Marcus had he fallen and scraped a knee. She took no offense at this liberty, simply leaned into his strength with gratitude.

"Don't you fret, Miss Brunel." His voice rumbled in his chest under her ear. "We're going to roll out the big guns. And then we'll see who runs, who fights, and who's left standing."

SOMETHING BIG STRUCK *Thetis*'s hull and wrenched a shriek of terror out of Georgia. She lost her footing and stumbled against the navigation table. For an endless minute she froze, gasping, gripping it with both hands, her gaze unable to leave the glowing prospect of Venice below her as the sky lightened toward dawn. She fully expected to see the earth begin its rush toward her as the airship fell into a long descent.

But no, the opposite was happening. The islands and bridges of Venice dropped steadily away, her view widening to show more and more of the Veneto as *Thetis* finished her turn and began to steam steadily west.

Or mostly west. The compass indicated she was headed west by north. At this rate they would wind up in Paris.

Georgia gabbled a prayer of thanks that she was still in the air, still functioning. Now, if the little ship just had enough water and coal to carry her to Geneva, she would ask nothing more of her Creator.

"*Thetis*, correct your heading. Set course due west, please, for Geneva. I know you know where that is." Everyone traveling across Europe was required to file a flight plan with Geneva, and smaller ships were required to moor for inspection before they went farther. The Alps could not be attempted without someone knowing where you were, and that you were flying in an airworthy vessel. The massive airfield was also in neutral Switzerland, where she could enlist help for her friends.

The little ship wobbled, as though its helm were stuck, and continued west by north without changing course.

"Oh, dear." She leaped for the wheel. "*Thetis*, give me the helm."

The wheel promptly unlocked its position and she spun it to a heading due west.

Thetis did not obey.

And then Georgia realized what had happened. "We've been hit, you goose," she told herself over the sinking feeling in her stomach. "The rudder and perhaps a vane are damaged. Now what are you going to do?"

Thetis was headed west by north. Did that mean the rudder could still work if she did not demand it go west? Her choices were limited. She could not go south to Rome, for her situation would not be much changed, and she knew no one there to whom she could appeal for help. East was out of the question—the Hapsburgs were no friends to England.

Hardly daring to hope, she spun the helm north.

Obediently, *Thetis* swung on to the new heading, the viewing ports in the bow showing her the great peaks of the Alps glinting in the distance as the first rays of the sun struck their lofty snows.

"North," she said. "Very well. We shall fly ourselves home to Munich, and raise the alarm with people who know the Thornes and will help them. *Thetis*, take the helm. I had better send a flight plan to Geneva so someone, at least, knows where I am. Otherwise I shall be arrested *again,* for stealing a registered vessel. I hope Teddy never finds out his mother is a fugitive from the law several times over."

Back in the communications cage, she had just sent the pigeon when a flash of an idea presented itself to her in all its glory. "Good heavens, Georgia, what a dunce you are!" She seized another sheet of message paper. "By now Signore Airone will have told Millie how you left the house. She thinks you are at the *questura!*"

She began to write so furiously the pencil was dull by the time she finished.

6:55 a.m.

Marcus being the closest thing to a host that *Foresight* possessed, he had done the honors, and showed Cora and her mother into one of the guest cabins close to his, so that they could have a wash and as much of a sleep as the rest of the night would allow.

He was awakened by the sun poking a blinding ray in through his porthole. He'd forgotten to slide shut the door of his sleeping cupboard. While it was his assigned cabin, it was just a fact that it just wasn't his bedroom at the hacienda in the Territory, so maybe he could be forgiven for forgetting details like that. Dad had told him, hadn't he? When they were in flight, it was important to roll shut the door so he wouldn't be chucked out on the floor if they ran into stormy weather.

But there was no weather here. Just another sunny day on an island the size of a fuselage, with nothing but lagoon on every side.

He dressed quickly and jogged down the corridor toward the dining saloon. What were the odds of there being anything fit to eat? They'd been in Venice for what seemed like weeks, and the crew had probably emptied the larder of provisions and taken it with them so as not to waste it. He'd probably have to siphon water out of the boiler to drink.

On the good side, he rather liked the idea of fishing for their breakfast. Surely Mr van Meere would have a rod and tackle somewhere—the man couldn't spend *all* his time designing mechanical devices. He must have a hobby that didn't include cogs and gears.

The dining saloon was empty, except for a fine view of Murano in the distance, and much closer to, a weathered tree trunk on the beach, on which egrets and cormorants were clustered, pecking and calling insults to one another. No food on the sideboard, or in it, for that matter.

But at the end of the table, on Mr van Meere's chair—a large affair where he took his solitary meals—there lay a neat brown egg.

Excellent! He liked eggs. Marcus couldn't imagine how it had got there, but he knew the cupboard in the galley where they were supposed to be.

The second surprise of the morning was finding Lady Thorne in the galley. Cora was seated at the worktable snapping thin planks of hardtack into pieces manageable for eating.

"Good morning, darling," Lady Thorne said cheerfully as he came in with the egg. "Were you able to rest?" She was opening cupboards and closets in a way he'd been expressly forbidden to during the flight across the Atlantic. Mr van Meere's personal chef and his cleaver had made it very clear that small boys were not welcome in his domain, no matter how hungry they were.

"Monsieur Lepine won't like you going through his cupboards like that, ma'am. We're not even allowed in here."

"Monsieur Lepine won't like finding three desiccated skeletons in his galley, either, should we not be able to locate something to eat during our stay," she responded.

Humph. She'd clearly never met Monsieur Lepine. He'd probably chuck their bones in a pot and make soup.

"Aha! Tinned goods. We are in luck, my dears. Marcus, do tell me there is a proper pantry somewhere."

He pointed at the deck-to-ceiling cupboard that she had not yet examined. The holy of holies, it was. Entry on pain of death. He scooted closer to look as she swung the doors open, half expecting it to be booby-trapped.

With a happy sigh, Lady Thorne took it in. No booby trap. Only bags of rice and noodles. Jars of sauces, both sweet and savory. A veritable mountain of bars of chocolate. Wheels of cheese. Eggs.

He put his contribution in the neat egg rack bolted to an inner wall. "I found it in the dining room," he explained, in case she might think he had stolen it.

"Did you, now? How did it get there, I wonder?"

He shrugged. "Is there enough here for breakfast? I could see if there's a fishing rod. We could have fresh fish."

"The second best idea I have heard all morning. Cora, darling, cease and desist with that horrible hardtack. Put it back in its tin and save it for when we really are desperate. We have enough to be going on with here."

"I want to go fishing, too," Cora announced, dumping the hardtack back in the tin and causing no damage to it at all.

"Off you go, then. I will complete my inventory of supplies. And see about a cup of coffee. The man is a Texican. He must have it somewhere about."

"In Bavaria, they drink coffee in the morning, like they do here," Cora told Marcus as they ran through the dining room. "I think it's vile, but she likes it. Oh, look. Another egg."

So there was, on the carpet leading into Mr van Meere's study. Marcus picked it up and put it in the bowl on the sideboard for safety. "A sea bird must have got in here somehow," he said. "I can't imagine eating a cormorant's eggs, though, can you? They must taste fishy."

"We might have to eat them," Cora said. "We don't know how long we'll be hiding out here."

At length they located the fishing rods in the last place he would have thought to look—the gun cabinet, next to Mr van Meere's study, where he kept a collection of hunting rifles. The egg lying on the carpet led him straight to it, like bread-crumbs in the forest, and when he picked it up and straightened, there were the rods in front of his face.

Cora took the eggs to the kitchen and then joined him on the beach, where he showed her how to bait the hook with a bit of dead fish he found under the egrets' roost. Casting was harder than he expected because of the light breeze, but on the other hand, there weren't any waves to speak of. In an hour they had hooked a mackerel and a bunch of smaller pilchards. He couldn't remember ever eating anything so good, once Lady Thorne filleted the fish, dredged in it flour and spices, fried it, and served it over fluffy rice with peas.

"We are a little low in the fresh vegetable department," she said apologetically. "I hope we can leave our hiding place before we get scurvy."

Marcus had no desire to get scurvy. Having the chicken pox when he was seven had been bad enough.

After they'd done the dishes and left the galley up to Mr Lepine's standards, he and Cora set off on a more extensive tour of the ship. "Don't forget, I want to learn to scale the fuselage like an aeronaut," she told him. "But meanwhile, do you suppose we ought to check the communications cage? Your father's employer may have messages."

"How are we supposed to get them to him?" Marcus wanted to know.

"Mama and I are in hiding. You're not," she reminded him. "If it was important, you could flag down a fishing boat."

He had to admit he probably could, and blame his presence on the islet on the neighborhood boys pulling a prank. He would take pleasure in naming them all.

They had almost reached the communications cage when somebody screamed.

Cora jumped and grabbed his arm. "What was that?"

Not a human. Not a cormorant. Cormorants and egrets croaked. In fact, that sound was about as familiar as could be. "I think we found where the eggs are coming from."

In an empty stateroom, two spotted hens lay near two

more eggs, using what seemed to be the last of their strength to cackle in weary satisfaction at this morning's achievement.

"For pity's sake," Cora said blankly. "Have they been here all this time?"

"They didn't come with us from the Territory, that's certain." He did some calculations and peered at them. "Only two or three days. Look. They've been in the water. Their feathers are all matted."

"The poor things. I wonder how far they had to paddle to get here."

They would never know. "They must have flown up *Foresight*'s chute where we got in. Look at them—they won't last another day. Let's get them some water and some of the leftover rice and fish."

The hens had clearly not eaten since they'd fetched up on the islet, and the rice and fish disappeared in seconds. Lady Thorne had smashed up some of the hardtack for them with a mallet, so they ate that, too, and drank a full bowl of water.

Revived by sustenance, and appearing to believe that he and Cora didn't mean to make a meal of them, the hens followed them out of the stateroom. "I suppose we had better check the communications cage," he said. "Then maybe the hens would like to go outside. There is a little grass to eat. Not much."

"Will you drop them down the chute?" Cora asked curiously as they pushed open the door.

"Of course not. Would you do that to a friend?"

She shook her head and held the door for the hens. "They're pretty. What shall we call them?"

"One and Two?" Marcus was a practical fellow, and it was

already clear who was first in the short pecking order. "This is Italy—maybe Prima and Secunda?"

"Goodness me, we can do better than that. How about Bella and Schatzi?"

One for beauty, and one for treasure. "Done. They'll learn quick enough who's who."

A ship this size had a dozen postal pigeons, though Marcus couldn't recall Mr van Meere sending more than one on the whole voyage from the Territory. He was a man of few words. But in the rack lay at least two that didn't belong to *Foresight*.

He opened the first to find a small package addressed to Mr van Meere. It didn't say URGENT on it, so that was something, and it was heavy. "Probably parts," he said over his shoulder, and put it back.

The second was a little smaller. Wait—

"What did you say the name of your ship was?"

"*Thetis*," Cora told him.

He held out the letter the pigeon contained. "Look."

With a quick intake of breath, she said, "We must take it to Mama at once. *Thetis* was—what's that word? Im—imp—"

"Impounded?"

"Yes! When Papa died. This may be important."

They hustled the hens out the door, and when they began to run down the corridor, the birds ran after them, using their wings to loft themselves to greater speed. They arrived in the galley in a great whirlwind of clucking and fuss.

Lady Thorne turned from the pantry in astonishment. "Good heavens. Are we under attack?"

"No," Marcus said. "This is Bella and Schatzi. They thought we were running away, not running to, and wouldn't be left behind."

"Mama, there was a pigeon from *Thetis*." Cora thrust the folded paper at her mother. "A letter for you."

"Impossible." She examined the name written on it. "I am supposed to be in hiding. Apparently I am doing a very poor job of it."

She unfolded the letter and read it aloud.

Dear Louise and Cora,

I hope desperately that this finds you somehow via Foresight. I am on my way to Munich in Thetis, for which I beg your forgiveness. I have stolen her from the Lido and in my escape I was fired upon. I will of course have the rudder and vanes repaired.

Millie will have discovered my absence last night and I cannot imagine how she must feel. Commissario Verdi did not take me to the questura, but directly to Minister del Campo, in whose employ he seems to be. Del Campo's only intent was to secure Cora, and with her in hand, to blackmail you into completing your work on the breakwater system. When I refused to divulge her location, he imprisoned me in his water dungeon beneath the palace, along with several skeletons of people who, like me, refused to give him what he wanted.

"Great snakes!" Marcus blurted, wide-eyed. He would have said more, except that they were ladies.

A kraken saved me. You must heap honors upon the head of your clever colleague who studied them. Using the electrical field, the creature put pictures in my mind that communicate both thought and memory, the way dreams do. In some of them I was able to see through its eyes. It was the most extraordinary experience of my life. The creature conveyed me through a tunnel and out into the open lagoon, where it swam me at speed to the Lido.

"Topping!" Agog, Cora did not seem to care that she was a lady. Her mother didn't even hear.

I hope that Millie is with you, or if not, that there is some way to inform her that I am safe. When I reach Munich, if I have not heard from you, I will solicit the Empress's assistance to extract you from Venice. I fear for your lives, and possibly that of Mr van Meere. The Doge and at least two of his ministers have no conscience when it comes to this plot for an independent kingdom. Foreigners are simply a means to an end.

I must close, as brave little Thetis is about to take on the Alps. I hope to hear from you shortly.

In haste,

Georgia Brunel

Blindly, Louise fumbled for a chair and fell into it. She read the letter a second time, and was starting on a third when Marcus could no longer contain himself.

"Lady Thorne!" He shook her arm and, dazed, she looked up. "We must tell Dad right away."

"About the krakens? Certainly. Good heavens, what a scientific breakthrough! The Imperial Biological Society must hear of this—my colleague must surely be admitted now."

"No!" Marcus howled in frustration. "Listen! Dad needs to know that Lady Langford is safe, and that Mr van Meere might be the next one the minister sticks in a water dungeon."

Her vision seemed to clear and when she looked at him, she saw him once again, not whatever fine pictures had been in her head. "I do apologize, Marcus. Of course you are right. But other than attempting to fly this behemoth and land it in the Piazza San Marco, how do you suggest we reach him?"

"A kraken," said Cora, as though this were the most obvious thing in the world. "Just as Lady Langford said, Mama. Marcus can wade out into the water and call one, I expect."

What a brilliant plan! Wouldn't those idiots in the street outside their house well and truly shut their faces when a kraken deposited him unharmed on the water stairs!

"They are not taxis, Cora," her mother said severely. "They are highly intelligent beings and are not at the service of humans unless they choose it. As Lady Langford has clearly demonstrated."

Marcus deflated with disappointment, then rallied as another thought struck him. He'd just go out while Lady Thorne was busy, and see if he could do it. Maybe a little one would come. What could he give it for a reward? What did krakens feed on, besides people?

Maybe they shouldn't have let the chickens eat all the left-over fish.

CHAPTER EIGHTEEN

*M*illie's knees felt like cooked linguine as Mr Seacombe knocked on the door of Mr van Meere's apartments. It swung open, and the big man glared out.

"What is it? I'm working."

Mr Seacombe, apparently, was used to his employer's rudeness—or perhaps he simply knew him better than to take the bluster at face value. "We have a problem, sir."

The glare faded by degrees as Mr van Meere seemed to sense that his bodyguard's grim face meant business. He waved them in. Belatedly, he observed there were two visitors in his foyer, not one. "Who's this, then?"

Millie lifted her chin. Mr Seacombe might have to put up with this man's manners, but she did not. "My name is Millicent Brunel. I am aunt by marriage to Georgia Brunel, Lady Langford, who is at present missing."

Cornelius van Meere was about the same height as Mr Seacombe, but easily twice his girth. His hair was curly, turning white at the temples, and standing up on end, as if fingers had been driven through it while trying to solve some equation of physics. He hadn't shaved today, and his cravat had been pulled askew. Grey eyes gazed out from under eyebrows formed like a cliff with birds' nests all along it.

"Brunel, you say? Any relation to the Thames tunnel man?"

"My uncle."

"Fine engineer. Met him once. A great loss to the world when he died."

"Lady Langford's son, Theodore Isambard Montgomery Brunel, fifth Baron Langford, is following in his footsteps," Millie informed him proudly. "He plans to lay a tunnel under the Channel to France."

For the first time, a ray of sunshine pierced the thundercloud. He gave a bark of laughter. "When he is ready to begin, I shall invest in the project. Well, come along in, and tell me about this problem."

Unlike Mr Seacombe's side of the courtyard, this side had clearly belonged to the noble family, not their staff. The ceilings were high and painted with frescoes of gods and goddesses, and the windows, which were at least eight feet tall and overlooked one of the wider canals, had been blocked by dressing screens, as though the present tenant feared people might be peering in from the villas opposite. Books, sheets of drawings, mechanical parts, and bits of clothing were strewn everywhere, and there appeared to be some kind of wheeled vehicle in a state of disarray in the dining room.

Her host saw her looking in at it as they passed. "Velocipede," he said. "Someone chucked it. Thought I could fix it, and I did. Helps me think when I'm stumped."

The sitting room did not appear to be in similar use, and it was even tidy. Millie was glad for it, as her skirts would be in no danger of engine grease as she sank on to the sofa. Mr Seacombe hitched a chair forward and launched into a bare-bones recitation of the events from the moment he had met Millie and Georgia. When he got to the part about Marcus and Cora being kidnapped, and the reason why, Mr van Meere raised a hand to stop him.

"Wait a minute. Let me get this straight. This murdered diplomat was Louise Thorne's husband?"

"Yep."

"And she is missing, too?"

"No, we know where she is," Millie said. "She is in hiding aboard *Foresight*. We sent her and Cora out there before dawn in a fishing boat."

He stared at her. "Louise Thorne is in Venice? On my ship? What the devil for?"

Seeing that she had put the cart before the horse in an effort to assure him Louise was safe, Millie handed the conversational reins back to Mr Seacombe.

He had got only a little further when his employer stopped him again. "Are you telling me that she and her daughter were here? In this house? And nobody told me?"

"It was for their safety," Millie said. "You were much occupied in meetings with the ministers, and we could not afford to let a single hint of their presence slip."

Mr van Meere swore, and Millie clamped her lips on the urge to remind him he was in the presence of a lady.

"What kind of buffoon do you take me for? I've known Louise Thorne since before she was married! D'you think I'm going to blab about her to anybody who asks?"

"You'd have no reason not to," Mr Seacombe said, apparently not much bothered by this display of temper. "But after three attempts to kidnap her daughter so they could dangle the child as bait to catch the mother, we couldn't take the chance."

Millie sat up straighter. "I should like your assurance that you will not divulge their location now."

"What in tarnation do you think would happen if I did?"

Mr Seacombe told him, blunt as a hammer. And then, as proof, he told him about the police taking Georgia away last night for no greater crime than for refusing to say where Cora was.

At last the big man was silent. Rearranging his notions, she had no doubt.

"So you see, sir, our connections have been disappearing at an alarming rate," Millie said. "Sir Francis is dead. The man who we believe to have killed him is dead. His wife and daughter are in hiding aboard *Foresight* with Marcus Seacombe. Lady Langford is missing, and I very much fear that the next person to disappear will be ... you. Or I."

He gazed at her. Even his eyebrows seemed to have calmed down at the gravity of their situation. "I see. Yes, I see now. It is a problem indeed."

Silence fell in the room. The walls of this elegant fortress were so thick that she could not hear the children playing outside, or even a gondolier calling to a friend across the canal.

Mr Seacombe shifted in his chair, and the movement seemed to rouse his employer from his reverie. "If I may ask, sir, how close to conclusion is your business in the Duchy?"

Mr van Meere made a noise of derision in his throat. "I've been wondering myself why things have ground to a halt. I've been kicking my heels here, playing with that velocipede while I doodled with the breakwater drawings and waited for the conference to begin. Now I see why it hasn't." His gaze moved to Millie. "They expected Lady Thorne there, too. And when they couldn't get her willingly, they fobbed me off with excuses while they tried to—" He paused.

"Get her unwillingly," Millie supplied.

He nodded. "Seacombe, I can see in your face what you want to do."

"Yep. Time to cast off ropes."

"It means the loss of millions, you know."

"You have millions, sir."

"I suppose I do. This project was more for amusement, really. To see if I could do it. But I didn't know I was being a party to all the rest of it. Kidnapping children. Coercing scientists. Making kings out of worms. It ain't right."

"Nope."

Mr van Meere sighed, then hooked a thumb over his shoulder in the direction of the mess in the other rooms. "Lucky I brought the plans back with me. These are the current originals. The copies they have are old versions, full of problems and without the adjustments Louise suggested when I was there a few months back."

"Better pack 'em up," Mr Seacombe said. "We ought to lift pronto."

"Not without Georgia!" Millie exclaimed. "Have you forgotten her already? How do you propose to get her out of the *questura*? Or will you simply leave me behind to kick my heels until the ambassador finds a barrister?"

"If she's still there, I'll eat my hat," Mr Seacombe said. "What are the odds the minister has her by now, to see if he can't lean more heavily on her?"

"Odds so good I wouldn't want to gamble," his employer responded. "He's a hard man to influence, though, del Campo is. Too used to having his own way. Everyone around him sees that he gets it, by fair means or foul."

Millie stood, clutching her reticule, unable to sit a moment longer. "Then we must employ foul means to have her returned. If it's these plans he wants, give them to him, for heaven's sake! If he values them more than his prisoner, it seems the obvious solution."

"And what's to stop him making Mr van Meere a permanent guest?" Mr Seacombe inquired. "One engineer in the hand is worth two in the bush."

"Mr van Meere isn't a defenseless bird," she snapped. "If anyone could fight his way out of a room full of politicians, he could."

Mr van Meere did not seem certain that this was a compliment.

"I don't advise your setting foot in that palace, sir, or in the *questura*, either," Mr Seacombe said. "We'll think of another way."

In Millie's mind, it had been an excellent plan, and he was just being stubborn because he hadn't thought of it. "What about your friend at the monastery?" If she must clutch at straws now, so be it. "Is he free to come and go in a house like that? Haven't they a chapel?"

With a frown, Mr Seacombe thought this over. "Might work. At least he could find out where Lady Langford is being held. If she really is in the house, the staff will know. If she's in lockup at the *questura*, we'll have to regroup. Been a long time since I engineered a gaolbreak."

He departed to see if his friend might lend his assistance.

221

Millie did not stay on Mr van Meere's side of the courtyard, but took her leave and busied herself tidying up the Seacombe side while she waited. There was not much to tidy, other than the breakfast dishes. Marcus had taken his rucksack with him, and when she dared peek into Mr Seacombe's room, it appeared that no matter how comfortably they were housed, father and son preferred to behave as though they might lift at a moment's notice. The large rucksack had either been packed that morning, or had never been unpacked at all.

By the time the sky was burned to a milky white by the noon sun, Millie was nearly prostrate from anxiety and fear that something had happened to Mr Seacombe now, too. She took up a watch in the courtyard at a little wrought-iron table. When she declined lunch, the signora brought her a plate of the hors d'oevres the Venetians called *cichetti*, and only the knowledge that she must keep up her strength and be ready for anything prompted her to eat them. But they tasted like straw in her mouth.

At length the big door creaked open, and thanks be to heaven, Mr Seacombe came in. But what had happened to him? Shoulders stooped, face white—he looked as though he had been stricken such a blow as would take him days to recover. Millie rose, her hands extended in case he needed assistance, but he shook his head.

"Upstairs," he croaked. "May as well both hear at once."

Mr van Meere must have been watching too, for the door opened and he hustled them inside. The mechanical parts still lay everywhere, but the rooms were bare of personal possessions. A trunk, a valise, and a portfolio that presumably held the plans stood waiting in the foyer. "Well? What happened, man? You look like death warmed over."

Mr Seacombe folded suddenly into a chair, as though his knees had given out. His employer poured a finger of amber liquid from a decanter on the sideboard and shoved it at him. "Drink it. No arguments."

After he did so, he gasped at the strength of the liquor, to which he clearly was not accustomed, and took a deep breath. "I'll be brief. My friend the monk confirmed that Lady Langford was at the minister's palace."

"Was?" Millie squeaked. "Is she somewhere else now?" For if they'd taken her to the prison adjacent to the Doge's palace, no power on earth but the barrister could save her. And how many years would that take?

"They imprisoned her in the water dungeon under the house. When this commissario went down to question her— again—" He choked, and had to recover himself before he went on. "After leaving her in the dark for a night and half a day, they lit the lamps and found her gone."

"Gone?" Mr van Meere repeated. "Be more specific, man."

"The water dungeon is just that. Some prisoners, apparently, are kept in cages suspended above the water. The ones he thinks will break more easily are put on platforms just above the surface."

"Then she has simply swum to safety," Millie said. "She can, you know. And sail, and ride to hounds, and pilot an airship. She is a woman of resources, and is hiding until she can escape, you may depend upon it."

Mr Seacombe passed a weary hand over his face. "No one can swim in those waters, ma'am. They are infested with krakens. The cook told my friend she likely lost her footing in the dark, and plunged in. No getting around it. She is dead."

"She most certainly is not!" Millie took a breath to tell him about the paper Lady Thorne's colleague had written, but he forestalled her with an upraised hand.

"There's more. On my way back here from the monastery, I passed the Villa dei Pappagalli. Two members of the *polizia* were at the door, talking with your Signore Airone."

"One tall and thin, one short and plump?" He nodded. "The Long and the Short of it. I wonder what they wanted?"

"Ma'am, consider," Mr van Meere said. "As far as they know, who is the only person left in Venice who might know where Cora is?"

If he had poured a pitcher of water on her head, it might have produced this cold, tingling shock at this unwelcome reminder.

"I cannot go back there," she whispered in acknowledgement. "But it is surely where Georgia will go, now that she has left the water dungeon."

"Miss Brunel—ma'am—" Mr Seacombe's eyes filled with sorrow.

"There is no need to look like an undertaker at a rainy grave," Millie said, beginning to recover her spirits as her mind worked through the possibilities. "We have nothing to fear from the krakens. I have it from Lady Thorne herself that they are capable of communicating with humans. Georgia has simply asked them for help, and escaped. Once she finds me not at home, it is likely she will come here. Therefore, with your permission, I will stay until she does."

She sat back upon the sofa with emphasis.

Mr van Meere and Mr Seacombe stared at one another. After a moment, the former said, "To perdition with it all. We'll lift within the hour. I can carry her if I have to."

"Yep," Mr Seacombe agreed.

Lift? Carry her? "I think not," she said. "How dare—"

Someone pounded on the door.

"Send her away," Mr van Meere said, thrusting both hands through his hair. "It's the signora with—"

Marcus burst through the door as though he'd been shot out of a cannon. "Dad! Dad! Lady Langford's in Munich and we have two chickens and we saw a baby kraken and— Hullo, Miss Brunel, what are you doing here?"

But Millie had only heard the first part. *"Georgia is in Munich?"* Astounded joy bubbled up inside her like a spring. She tossed a smug smile at the two unbelievers in the room. That would teach them to underestimate a Brunel. "Did the krakens help her escape?"

Marcus goggled at her as though she had just announced she could see ghosts and predict the future. "How did you know?"

Millie beamed at him. "Science."

The boy thrust a letter at his father. "Here. She sent a pigeon to *Foresight*. She swam with the krakens and got away and stole an airship!" From the sound of it, Georgia had become the boy's heroine overnight.

Both men read the letter, and then read it a second time. When it looked like a third was imminent, Millie snatched it out of their hands and read it herself. She folded it up and slipped it into her reticule. Some day, when she and Georgia wrote their memoirs, they would want it.

"That's that sorted," she said with satisfaction. "Now, I heartily agree that we must leave Venice before the Long and the Short of it come back to arrest me, or the minister's men come for you, Mr van Meere. I will return to the villa as quietly as possible and gather our things. In an hour you will find me ready at the water stairs, if you will be so kind as to include me on the journey out to *Foresight*? We must fly to Munich at once, of course, to collect my niece and take Lady Thorne and Cora home."

Mr van Meere's mouth was still opening and closing, as though too many things were trying to come out of it. Or perhaps he was simply not used to a woman telling him what to do.

Inclining her head in farewell, Millie saw herself out, to find Lorenzo waiting down the street at the public water stairs.

"The boy has told you all?" he asked, getting the gondola underway before Millie had fairly seated herself.

"Yes. I must pack as quickly as I can. Mr Seacombe and his party will collect me in an hour."

"My grand-uncle stands ready near Saluté. It is the wrong time of day for fishing, but he will convey you all out into the lagoon more discreetly than a vaporetto would."

"Shall we have to cover ourselves with canvas?"

Lorenzo did not smile. "I think it is too late for that, Signorina."

CHAPTER NINETEEN

*O*nce again, Lorenzo's grandmother demonstrated her talent for deception. She dressed Millie in an ancient set of widow's weeds and a heavy veil. Black crepe was draped over their trunks and valises in the gondola, and, the vaporetto idea having been abandoned, Mr Seacombe and Mr van Meere switched to black jackets and were loaned Venetian men's mourning caps with flat tops. Marcus hid under the crepe, children not being a normal part of a cortège.

The sad procession moved much more quickly than such things were wont to do, however. Men on the bridges barely had time to remove their hats before the gondolas were under and steering up the canal as though the widow might be late for the funeral.

Millie did not dare remove the hot, heavy veil until they were past Saluté and well into the mouth of the Grand Canal. As they spotted the fishing boat, the church bells began to ring, that urgent sound that meant the bridges were going up, peals entirely different from the call to worship. She turned in her seat to watch the movement of the neighborhoods on the great gearworks, only to hear Lorenzo give a shout.

"Grab hold, Signorina! The wakes! My grand-uncle must brave them before we are swept away!"

Gripping the seat, Millie faced forward to see the little fishing boat steaming toward them at full speed. Behind them, a wave like a tidal bore was already forming. So this was what happened when the neighborhoods moved. It all looked so exciting and quaint from the villa—she had never once thought of what might happen out in the lagoon. No wonder the krakens were so irritated with the poor prisoners cleaning the gears. An operating clockwork city was probably the last thing the creatures wanted to live with.

The boat reduced pressure and steamed up beside them. Someone threw down a rope ladder, someone else a net for the luggage. But before Lorenzo could boost her up the ladder, the wave struck. He lost his footing and fell backward into the gondola.

The gondola rocked—bucked—and with a shriek, Millie went over the side.

The lagoon's waters closed over her head and she watched the borrowed veil come off and float toward the sunlight. Her feet and billowing skirts blotted out the sun and she distinctly heard the hull of the fishing boat creak as it withstood the wash of the wave.

And then something wrapped around her arm.

Paralyzed with terror, she could do nothing, not even breathe, as the tentacle pulled her closer, through water that seemed to be spangled with fireflies, to a forest of tentacles—large, thick, the color of burgundy wine. Her wide eyes met that of a creature from a book—or a dream—an eye on each side of a helmet-shaped head. The small tentacle touched the bare skin of her hand (where had the black lace gloves gone?) and tapped it.

The moment she opened her hand, pictures flooded her head—a tunnel, a blonde girl smiling—Georgia—the underwater sands of an island.

Georgia, she thought in a moment of glad recognition. *My family.* Somehow, even as her lungs compressed for lack of air, she had the sense to add, *Thank you.*

A moment later, she got a mouthful of the sea as she was thrust upward and tipped back into the gondola as suddenly as she'd fallen out of it. Blinded, coughing, she could not see who grabbed her by the skirts and thrust her upward a second time, but she felt rope under her hands. A moment later she was hauled over a very hard gunwale like a tuna and landed on the deck with a splash.

"Miss Brunel!" a gravelly voice said urgently. "Are you hurt? Can you speak?"

"Force the water out of her," Mr van Meere said, and the same hands seized her around the ribs.

It was this shocking indignity that make her squeak and recover her dazed senses. "I am—perfectly—well!" she gasped.

On hands and knees, head hanging down, she coughed up the seawater and at last could breathe. She felt the deck vibrate as the fishing boat laid on steam, and tried to remember where her feet were.

Too many clothes. "Get me out of these weeds!"

It was Marcus—who had not yet learned too much propriety—who helped her. "Miss Brunel, the kraken saved you! Oh, it was topping. Did you speak to it? We thought you lost and drowned and the next minute, half a dozen tentacles tipped the gondola and chucked you back in. Do they really speak?"

"No," she managed, struggling out of the heavy bombazine skirts, now ruined beyond repair. "They put pictures in your head. Be careful with the hooks, darling." Off came the stiff whaleboned bodice and she gasped with relief. "But I did manage to thank it—or its kind, at least—for saving Georgia. I believe it understood."

"Ripping!" Marcus said with stark admiration. "I say, Dad, this trip is as good as anything An Educated Gentleman ever wrote!"

"Are you sure you're all right?" Mr Seacombe looked as though he was about to be sick. "Miss Brunel, I haven't got words for how glad I am you were not drowned."

"And I can't express how glad I am Lady Thorne told us about the krakens. They really do not mean us harm. They have more to fear from humans." She got to her feet and clutched the gunwale to look back the way they had come. "Is it over? Has the city stopped moving?"

"Seems like." Beside her, Marcus peered over the gunwale. "But what's that?"

A tiny shape detached itself from the receding vista of buildings and jetties, a ribbon of steam streaming away behind its stack. Whatever it was, it was moving at speed.

"Is that a vaporetto?" she asked. "I did not know they could travel so fast."

Mr Seacombe drew in a sharp breath through his nostrils. He shouted something at Lorenzo's grand-uncle, and in a moment, a great gout of steam issued from their own stack and the decks vibrated harder. Waves began to slap at the bow.

"What is it?" Blast the wind and the drying salt in her eyes. She could not see!

"That's no vaporetto," he said grimly. "That is the *polizia*. The jig is up. They are in pursuit."

Millie raked hair and salt out of her face and turned for the bow. And there it was, the airship *Foresight*, looking like a grey thundercloud swelling over an islet that seemed too tiny to hold it up. "My goodness!" she said in spite of herself. Nobody except the Albion Line could possibly need a ship that big. What was it transporting besides one millionaire and his crew?

And then Marcus exclaimed, "Dad! She's under steam! What's Captain Torkelsen doing?"

Mr van Meere shouted a phrase that definitely should never have been heard by a lady or a child.

For *Foresight* was definitely under steam, and what's more, five of the six mooring ropes were already cast off. As they watched, the last came free, the gangway went up, and the ship lifted gently into the air.

"She's lifting!" Marcus shouted. "Is she leaving without us? Hey! Cora! Wait for us!"

Millie half expected the great ship to turn tail, but of course they wouldn't. Their millionaire employer was standing on the deck swearing like an aeronaut, half soaked from hauling Millie in. It made way toward them, and suddenly she understood.

"They've seen the pursuit," she shouted, and whacked him on the arm to get his attention. "They're going to lower a basket so Lorenzo's grand-uncle can make his escape, too!"

"A basket?" Mr van Meere repeated, his voice rising. "On

the open sea? I'll have Torkelsen's head for this, blast him all to blazes!"

Whatever his employer was paying *Foresight*'s captain, it wasn't enough, for he had clearly divined that to bring the fishing vessel in to the islet and get everyone and the luggage off would cost more time than they had. He brought the massive ship in above them as gently as a bit of thistledown, and as their fishing boat reduced pressure and slowed, down came the rescue basket. Instead of merely holding two or three people, one could have rescued a steam landau in the blessed thing. Millie and Mr van Meere and the luggage, Mr Seacombe and his rucksack, and Marcus could roll about in it like marbles.

And they did, for it rose with alarming speed, forcing Millie to her knees before she was knocked down, where she clutched a strap for dear life and watched the hatch approach above. The basket locked in its berth and a young man offered her a hand to assist her out of it. With a glance over her shoulder, she saw that the fishing boat was already out of sight behind the islet, and steaming northeast across the lagoon toward an archipelago that would, she hoped, conceal it long enough for Lorenzo and his grand-uncle to elude their pursuers.

The deck pressed up under Millie's soaked boots, and they fell blithely into the sky.

Something metal pinged off the hull.

Mr Seacombe plucked Marcus out of the basket by main force and hustled them both down a very fine teak-lined corridor.

"Marcus!" Cora came running to meet them. "Isn't it exciting? They tried to shoot at us! The first engineer is laughing at them. I suppose that means he has stopped being so angry at Mama."

"What's he angry for?" Marcus wanted to know.

"She made him ignite the engines. And what a fuss the captain made about it! But you know, even the Empress can't make Mama stop when she wants something, and she wanted to lift, so we did."

"So it's her head Mr van Meere wants on a pike, then." Millie smiled over her shoulder at that gentleman, lumbering along behind them and looking positively thunderous.

"Louise has no business bossing my crew around," he grumbled. "'Tisn't fitting."

"On the other hand, she did save our lives," Millie pointed out. "Or at least, saved us from a visit to the water dungeons, once the *polizia* were finished with us."

"I suppose," he grumbled. "Is there any grub on this boat?"

"Oh yes," Cora said. "The crew brought ever so much. Monsieur Lepine is busy in the galley, and he said to tell you that whiskey and wine and cake are laid out in the saloon."

"Cake?" Marcus looked alarmed. "Does anyone know where Bella and Schatzi have got to? You didn't lift without them, did you?"

"Who?" Mr van Meere said.

"'Course not," Cora retorted. "But still—you may be right—"

As one, the two children pelted off in the direction of, Millie presumed, the saloon.

She, however, was escorted to a stateroom even finer than the one she had briefly occupied aboard *Juno*, where she bathed and dressed and arranged her hair in a manner fit to appear in public. Her wet clothes had already been borne away to be laundered, she saw as she crossed to the generously sized viewing port. Goodness. It was like staying at the Ritz—or at least, she imagined it would be.

Clouds sailed over the countryside below them, and ahead, she could see the gleaming peaks of the Alps. Munich lay just on the other side.

Munich, and dear Georgia, waiting for them. Safe and well.

Millie sent a prayer of thanks into the vaults of heaven. For the krakens, bless them. For two children's irrepressible bravery and spirits. For Lady Thorne and Mr Seacombe. And for Mr van Meere and his ostentatious, life-saving ship.

But mostly, she gave thanks for friendship. And love.

And for the family that had brought her both.

May 11, 1895 at 5:30 p.m.

Georgia was too well-bred to fidget, so instead she paced up and down in the grass of the Theresienwiese, the great field outside Munich where the people held their October festival. *Thetis* was moored at the city airfield, reasonable and modest vessel that she was, having her rudder and vanes repaired. Empress Christina, horrified by what had happened to her favorite engineer, was footing the bill and expecting *Foresight*'s entire company to wait upon her at their earliest convenience.

Empress Christina, needless to say, was in a temper about the Duchy's treatment of the Thorne family. It was all Georgia could do to restrain her from leaping into an airship and dropping bombs upon the Duchy in person. This, Her Imperial Majesty was eventually brought to see, was no way to solve a diplomatic tangle. She had ambassadors for that.

Far above, something blotted out the late afternoon sun.

Georgia's pulse broke into a canter as *Foresight*'s massive fuselage grew larger and larger on its final approach, until at last the ship settled on the grass forty feet away from the large steam-powered estate vehicle in which Georgia had arrived.

The Kastanienhof driver muttered something roughly translated as "by great Odin's curly beard" as he took in the size of it.

The gangway was still six inches off the ground when Marcus and Cora flew down it (figuratively speaking) followed by two speckled hens (literally speaking).

"Auntie Georgia!" Cora slammed into her embrace. "Oh, I am so glad to see you. We thought you were dead and then we got your letter and—"

Marcus hugged her, too. "Dad was beside himself and Miss Brunel fell in the lagoon and talked to a kraken and—"

"—it's my birthday and coming home is the best present ever!"

Georgia laughed and disentangled herself, but still the children did not let go of her hands. "I had not forgotten the date, darling. I have been to Kastanienhof and left it in a whirlwind of preparations for your homecoming. Frau Brucker is at this moment making your favorite cake. Marcus, how did you come by those hens?"

"They came by us. They were inside *Foresight* when we got there." He beamed proudly at the hens, who were busy pulling worms out of the grass and nipping off the tops of the blades. "Aren't they fine? Mr van Meere says I may keep them."

"I should say so," Cora told him. "And if he changes his mind, I shall give them a home at Kastanienhof."

Laughing, Georgia left the children and the hens in the shadow of the fuselage. Millie was trying not to hurry down the gangway, and failing miserably, so Georgia met her at the foot of it with an enormous hug.

It was all she could do not to weep with relief that Millie was safe—which was difficult when Millie herself was weeping into her shoulder. "I thought—you were dead." Millie mastered herself with the help of a handkerchief.

"The krakens—"

"Yes, the wonderful, terrifying creature told me. I took the opportunity to thank it for saving you."

"You blessed dear." Georgia hugged her again, and resolutely did not notice Mr Seacombe strolling down the gangway, his gaze upon her. "Come, everyone. We are expected for supper at Kastanienhof."

"Good heavens," Lady Thorne said, raising her eyebrows in astonishment as the driver opened his ungainly steam vehicle's doors for them. "You haven't brought the farm dray?"

"It was either that or commandeer a train," Georgia explained. "I would have come in *Thetis*, but the Empress is having her repaired for you. I do apologize for not getting her out of the way of the Lido cannons in time, but it couldn't be helped."

Louise nodded, as though it did not signify. "I would fly with you through a fusillade, you brave woman. Cora—Marcus—ask the hens to join us, please, and for goodness sake keep hold of them as we travel. They may join ours in the poultry yard tonight."

The journey to Kastanienhof was both short and noisy

with chatter. When an equally noisy but much longer supper was over, Cora sighed with happiness as her birthday cake was brought in by Frau Brucker, who was wreathed in smiles now that what remained of her household was safely at home.

"Pflaumkuchen," Cora explained to Marcus. "Plum cake. She knows I love it above anything else, even hazelnut torte."

The children were bundled off to a well-earned rest afterward, while the adults settled in the Thorne sitting-room with its view of the lake and the mountains beyond. In the distance, Munich twinkled in the falling dusk as each party brought the others up to date.

"Can't fathom how a man could stoop to such evil," Mr Seacombe remarked with a shake of his head. He took another sip of the fine port Louise had poured for them all.

"By looking too high, I suspect," Millie said with her uncanny ability to put her finger upon the heart of the matter.

"But to resort to kidnapping, extortion, and murder?" Mr van Meere's terrifying eyebrows beetled into a frown. "The man's a worm—all of them, a tangle of worms. They deserve each other."

"I do not speak for you, of course, Cornelius, but I for one will not be returning to Venice in this lifetime," Louise said. "Nor will I have any part in any engineering project the Duchy may be involved in, no matter how interesting it is."

"Agreed," he said gruffly. "They may use my old plans and see how far they get." He glanced up at her, the brows lifting as a thought occurred to him. "I never did fix that problem with the flood prevention mechanism."

"Dear me." Millie looked a little alarmed. "Has Venice not enough trouble with flooding?"

"It will not harm the city," he assured her. "But the weight of the water will make the cogs fail. The ones that cause the sections to close." He shook his head at himself. "Foolish mistake. Embarrassing."

Louise came close to a triumphant grin. "We may not have succeeded in giving Minister del Campo and that appalling *commissario* their just deserts, but at least we may find some satisfaction in making the former a national embarrassment. Perhaps he may even lose his post."

"Oh, happy thought," Georgia said lightly.

All the same, it would be a long time before she could sleep without those flat, soulless eyes haunting her nightmares.

Louise offered the use of her steam landau to transport the gentlemen back to the festival field, where they would sleep aboard *Foresight*. "I am not hurrying you off," she assured them. "But I want to look in on the children, and I do not want to fall asleep on my feet while I do so."

"I'll be back in the morning for Marcus," Mr Seacombe said. "And the hens," he added belatedly, as though remembering that his family had increased by two.

"We lift no later than noon," Mr van Meere said as they all walked outside. "Give the Empress my regrets. I have a powerful need to see the deserts and mesas of home again, after this. Your contract, Seacombe, is fast approaching its conclusion. Guess you won't be too unhappy about that."

Mr Seacombe said nothing as his employer lumbered off with Louise to the carriage house. Millie took her leave of him with a quiet, heartfelt shake of the hand before retiring upstairs.

He and Georgia stood in the gravel sweep. The May evening was soft with the scent of lilacs and soil and newly mown grass ... and the feeling that something was about to happen. The way one could smell snow coming, or feel thunder before it rumbled.

Mr Seacombe cleared his throat. "Well, I guess this is good-bye. Won't see much of you tomorrow. I'll just collect my boy and his hens, and be off."

"I suppose it is."

He was silent a moment. "Will I see you again, my lady?"

The two words were a caress.

"I do not know." Oh, why would this shivery feeling not cease and desist? She was trembling like a debutante at her first ball. "I feel unable to divine the future any farther than tomorrow. Louise, Millie, and I must wait upon the Empress, to tell her what happened."

"Perhaps you might want to travel farther afield someday."

What did he mean? Farther than what? "I was thinking of France," she said, to fill the confused silence. "I have a friend in Provence, at the Château Valmy. She was at the exhibition, and extended the invitation."

"You have friends in the Territories now, too."

"But—but they have not invited me."

"They have now. We're on a ranch north of Santa Fe, not too far from Mr van Meere's spread. Couple hundred acres on the Pecos River. Nothing but piñon pine, Navapai herds, and red rocks as far as the eye can see. It's at your disposal any time you want to come and paint it."

Though the twilight was too deep now for him to observe it, she felt the scalding heat of a blush in her cheeks. The lamps of the landau glimmered out from between the chestnut trees and the sound of gravel crunching under its wheels reached them.

"Perhaps I shall," she managed.

But she didn't think he heard her, for he had started forward to meet the vehicle. Louise got out, they shook hands, and Seacombe took his place in the pilot's chair, his employer beside him.

A moment later, he lifted his hand in farewell, pushed the acceleration bar forward, and rolled away down the long avenue of chestnut trees.

Georgia stood there in the scented, gentle evening. She did not move for some time, even after the singing sound of the landau had faded into a memory.

EPILOGUE

MAY 11, 1895 AT 8:10 P.M.

*C*ommissario Verdi cursed the purple evening, the new route he had to take home from the *questura*, and the barely familiar lanes and canals between himself and the modest dome of San Sebastiano, in whose shadow he lived. Every time the neighborhoods changed it took him at least a day to recreate a morning and evening route, despite the fact that he was a Venetian by birth and blood.

Of course he could wave down a gondola, or use a vaporetto hired at the bigger crossings. But that would cost money, and he never spent money when he could do a job himself. Perhaps that was why Maria had deserted him. He snorted. She could go to the devil. Probably had, without him to look after her.

And so could the two idiots who had managed to lose Millicent Brunel. The single source of information on Cora Thorne's whereabouts—the one route to getting Louise Thorne into Venice and thence into Minister del Campo's hands. No one seemed to know where the Brunel spinster was—not the majordomo at the Villa dei Pappagalli, not the staff at the villa where Signore van Meere had recently been staying. That gentleman was rumored to be enjoying an affair with her. Perhaps they had quarreled, and could be why he'd departed so abruptly, abandoning his engagement to dinner at the minister's house. A wonderful meal and a bit of questioning had been on the menu.

The minister was not happy the wealthy tinkerer had been allowed to leave. Verdi could not understand why, when the plans for the breakwater had been delivered promptly to the minister's office. Nor was del Campo happy that the widow Brunel was dead, for now he would be troubled with formulating an explanation for that bumpkin, Sir Ernest Davies-Howe.

Verdi wasn't sorry Georgia Brunel was dead. He'd seen the drying puddles of seawater on the plinth where he'd put her, which told him instantly what had happened to the maddening woman. He'd disliked her on sight, though she was a toothsome bit of baggage. Titled, was she? Thought herself better than he, did she? Well, he'd had the last laugh, even if it had cut off a line of investigation. Luckily there was this other Brunel—or there would be, just as soon as he located her.

With the minister's kind permission, an hour ago he'd put his two officers on the same stone plinth. A day or two stewing in their own fear served a dual purpose. It would punish them for their failure to bring in Millicent Brunel, and it might squeeze something useful out of them—some memory, some half-forgotten word or reference that might give him a new path to Lady Thorne. While they were there, he'd start hauling in the staff of the two villas, beginning with the Airones. They were hiding something, he knew it. It had been a long time since one of his hunches had been wrong, and the old lady had an air of triumph that did not bode well for her during questioning.

Verdi lifted his head and recognized nothing around him in the neighborhood. He sighed. A walk up the steps of the nearest bridge for a sighting of the dome reassured him he had not wandered too far off the most direct course. A right turn at the base of the bridge, and a walk along the *fondamente* to the bar he could see in the distance would put him within a few hundred yards of home.

No one was about except for the people spilling out of the lamplit bar. Maybe he should stop in for a drink and some *cichetti*. Save having to forage for something at home. Decision made, he took a step forward, already anticipating a glass of grappa and some broiled *polpi* rolled up in lettuce and herbs.

Something tugged on his trouser leg and his stride became an awkward hop as he fought to keep his balance. Was he caught on a nail?

He looked down, another curse forming on his tongue, to see a reddish tentacle wrapped around his ankle.

A sound not unlike the howling of a dog echoed across the canal, and he realized with horror it had come out of his own mouth. "Get off! Off!" He tried to stamp on the tentacle, but the only result was another one slithering up to wrap around his other ankle.

Was he dreaming? The krakens never came up the canals. Too many people with spears and flintlocks. Where was his? His hands flailed at his belt even as the tentacles flexed and jerked his feet out from under him. He crashed on the stone *fondamente* so hard it knocked the breath out of him, and in the next moment, the creature had pulled his helpless body over the lip and into the water.

Deep water. Disgusting canal water.

He could see nothing. Couldn't breathe. He clamped his lips tightly shut so the water wouldn't enter his body.

Lights began to flicker all around him, and his bowels loosened as a large, soulful eye in a hellish head floated out of the darkness. Something tapped his hand. When it went boneless with fear and opened, pictures flashed in his mind. Prisoners on the gearworks. Himself, forcing some criminal out of a bubble, only to have the man borne away by a yellow kraken. A blonde girl, smiling. Himself again, this time in a cage suspended from a chain and passing over the creature's head, his face clearly lit by the lantern. That aggravating Brunel woman, seen from below, on the plinth, her eyes piteous as the light faded.

A bright flare of hatred burned through him, as searing as the lack of air in his lungs. It was her fault! She had brought him to this pass. Every humiliation and inconvenience he had endured since yesterday was down to her.

The kraken flowed into motion—traveling along the bed of the canal with him wrapped in its arms like a baby. Its speed astonished him—or would have, if the blue lights hadn't somehow transferred themselves into his head. Dazzled him. Hurt him.

His mind was giving way. His lungs were compressing.

Can't—breathe—hail Mary, full of grace—

The kraken took him past the gearworks that moved the city's neighborhoods, then deeper, to the very bed of the lagoon two hundred feet down, where weeds waved in the currents and fish flashed among them. When it reached the massive foundation on which the city rested, it released him.

He might have been awed had he been alive to see it. But he had drowned before they cleared the Grand Canal, and it would be some days before his body, identifiable only by the beautifully chased flintlock, a family heirloom still in its holster, would be recovered.

The work of assassins, of course. Commissario Verdi had many enemies.

Most regrettable. But this was Venice, the clockwork city, and such was only to be expected.

THE END

AFTERWORD

I hope you have enjoyed *The Clockwork City*, and our new adventures in the Magnificent Devices world via the Lady Georgia Brunel Mysteries. Georgia and Millie's adventures will continue in book two, *The Automaton Empress*. If this is your first visit to my alt-history world, I hope you will begin your adventures with the first books in my three connected steampunk series:

- *The Emperor's Aeronaut (The Regent's Devices 1, 1819)*
- *Lady of Devices (Magnificent Devices 1, 1889)*
- *The Bride Wore Constant White (Mysterious Devices 1, 1895)*

I invite you to visit shelleyadina.com to subscribe to my newsletter, browse my blog, and learn more about my books. Or visit moonshellbooks.com to buy directly from me.

Welcome to the flock!

Warmly,

Shelley

ALSO BY SHELLEY ADINA

Brilliant Devices

A Lady of Resources

A Lady of Spirit

A Lady of Integrity

A Gentleman of Means

Devices Brightly Shining (Christmas novella)

Fields of Air

Fields of Iron

Fields of Gold

Carrick House (novella)

Selwyn Place (novella)

Holly Cottage (novella)

Gwynn Place (novella)

Acorn (novella)

Aster (novella)

Iris (novella)

Rosa (novella)

The Regent's Devices series with R.E. Scott

The Emperor's Aeronaut

The Prince's Pilot

The Lady's Triumph

The Pilot's Promise

The Aeronaut's Heart

ABOUT THE AUTHOR

Shelley Adina is the author of more than 50 novels published by Harlequin, Warner, Hachette, and Moonshell Books, Inc., her own independent press. She writes steampunk adventure and mystery as Shelley Adina; as Charlotte Henry, writes classic Regency romance; and as Adina Senft, is the *USA Today* bestselling author of Amish women's fiction.

She holds a PhD in Creative Writing from Lancaster University in the UK. She won RWA's RITA Award® in 2005, and was a finalist in 2006. She appeared in the 2016 documentary film *Love Between the Covers*, is a popular speaker and convention panelist, and has been a guest on many podcasts, including Worldshapers and Realm of Books.

When she's not writing, Shelley is usually quilting, sewing historical costumes, or enjoying the garden with her flock of rescued chickens.

Shelley loves to talk with readers about books, chickens, and costuming!

www.shelleyadina.com
shelley@shelleyadina.com